KUSUM

DR KHALIL ISAAC MATHAI

Made with ♥ on the Notion Press Platform
www.notionpress.com

Kusum:

The insistent niggle of a reluctant alarm nudged her awake. Kusum stretched and shivered before hopping out of bed. Groggily, she opened the window blinds. A mist of cool air wafted in through the half-open window panes. The courtyard was coming awake. Slivers of sunlight probed the foliage, prizing chaperoning shadows apart. Kusum squinted through the shredded mist and dewdrops on the glass panes of her first-floor bedroom. Two parrots attacked an overripe mango on the tree outside. The dogs were back, exhausted after a night of vigilance patrol. They lay flopped in synchronized symmetry in familiar slots outside the ancestral house. A squirrel scurried up a coconut tree in a vivid display of athletic panache. Butterflies flitted across the lawn. The old house, uninhabited at night, shimmered in dewy anticipation of human warmth. The house, a heirloom of the Thoppil family would come alive with kitchen fires and contemporary intrigue soon. The rambling dining space in the old structure was flanked by two bedrooms, a kitchen, and a study. Perched atop, with a ladder leading up from the study, was a loft. Kusum often wondered what lay in the loft.

The old house with its silent sorrows and stubborn resilience reflected the ethos of an era past. Built a couple of hundred years ago, the construct reflected toil, resilience, and the shadows of violence of a bygone era. In those days, land was pristine, rich, and available. Families and businesses were founded and fortunes flourished on fortitude, agriculture, ferocity, and trade. Those were wild and violent days. Opportunities and evil lay enmeshed in the collage. Murderous robbers lurked and murky secrets lay buried in the shadows. The fiercest and the most bloodthirsty dacoits were the river pirates. In their fast arrow boats, they flitted betwixt the river's shadows praying upon unsuspecting, hapless houseboats and riverside houses. The prevalent, primal arm of law enforcement focused on taxation. The law did not have the time, reach, mandate, or inclination to protect private citizens. Each man guarded his house, his household, and his neighbours. There was safety in numbers. Houses were clustered together for security. Most men could and would wield a sword or an axe. A dacoit who was caught, faced draconian, decadent justice as brutal as the times.

Kusum was enthralled by the aroma, aura, and architecture of the ancestral house. The house had solid wood walls, barricaded windows, and doors reinforced with brass trappings. If you had the whim and fortitude to clamber up a clunky wooden ladder you could climb to the loft. The loft was the sanctum of old. If dacoits attacked, this was the last bastion of defence. You could hide and hold out here with your treasured possessions and women. Drawing up the ladder you could wait for help when other defences had crumbled. Now, the loft was not used. Spider webs, darkness, mystery, an old ladder, rats, and dust deterred debasing familiarity. The loft was the one part of her in-law's ancestral house Kusum had yet to explore. The opportune moment never came and her inclination to seek exacting excitement was in abeyance. Soon after she shifted to the Thoppil house, Kusum had decided that she would get the place cleaned up. The venture had been deferred indefinitely on a whim. There was no urge of expedience nor any whiff of compunction to tidy up the loft. It was not of any practical utility and languished unused by humans while rodents roamed unmolested. The family stayed in a new modern construct with shiny marble tiled floors, split air conditioning, and designer bathroom trappings.

Kusum was an engineer by training. She was astute in academics and ebullient by nature. At university, she had been a student union representative, a table tennis blue in sports, and a gold medallist in academics. Kusum had been married to Joseph of Thoppil's house a month ago. Her parents had considered it a good match. The boy's family was traditionally illustrious and the boy himself was nimble. Joseph had flitted through his engineering course. He surprised everyone and himself and surpassed peer expectations by passing the qualifying examinations. In his academic endeavors, projects, and presentations he was aided by some opportune if inappropriate assistance from experienced and well-tipped college attendants.

Both Kusum and Joseph merged into the throng of unemployed engineers. This was a time when there were few openings for graduates in India. The euphoria of independence had given way to a phase of economic doldrums, pork barrel appeasement politics, and socialist pretensions. The aspiration of emergent, enterprising Indian youth was to emigrate or to find a spouse who would assist them in emigrating. Joseph was resourceful. A dubious placement portal secured him a well-paid job in the Middle East.

Kusum stayed at home. Her campus credentials had opened windows of opportunity in academia and research. She, however, had not been allowed to work or to pursue her post-graduate aspirations. Her plans for education abroad had been squashed. An overqualified girl was an encumbrance for her family and an embarrassment in the marriage market. Kusum's parents were wary of her chutzpah. Her mother hoped that marriage would temper her pretensions and quell her exuberant aspirations. Kusum acquiesced to the inevitable. She had no desire to embarrass her family. An unmarried daughter was a liability. There would be furrowed brows in church and whispered insinuations from fossilized family friends.

Kusum appraised Joseph's house for the first time after her marriage. The house was an incongruent hybrid construct. An ancient solid structure took pride of place in the courtyard. To one side was a glitzy garish modern mini mansion with contemporary continental amenities and an attitude of contemptuous frivolous disdain. The old house had character. Unlike the cement and façade structure where they would stay, the old construct was a living, throbbing entity. Shimmering spider's webs and dust frosted over a bygone era's mysteries. Kusum could sense and sync with the old house's ethos. She could sense and savor the unheard cacophony of subdued and submerged hidden truths whispered by the woodwork. For the first time after her marriage was conceptualized and consummated, Kusum felt a thrill coursing through her veins. A glint of hope was ignited. The promise of adventure shimmered through the abyss of disdain she had been ensconced in by inappropriate matrimony. Within the portals of the old house, she sensed a growing camaraderie, a sense of ownership and belonging. Her destiny seemed intertwined with the house's lofts, granaries, and secret storage chambers. Joseph had no time for the old house. He considered the old house an embarrassment and an encumbrance. Joseph disliked the old house and all that it stood for. To him, the construct reflected the needs, culture, and lifestyle of a bygone era. Today, for Joseph, the house served no purpose and was an eyesore and a spectacular white elephant.

Theirs was an arranged marriage. Kusum met her prospective groom a week before the ceremonies. He had come to her house with his parents to 'see and size' the bride-to-be. Draped in a cling-wrapped chiffon sari and chuffed up with perfume and powder Kusum had been miserable. She was under orders to look pretty and to avoid intelligent conversation. Her parents were under no delusions about Joseph's intellect. If Kusum were to engage him in conversation with content, Joseph would flounder and abandon ship. The visit went true to the script. Joseph's dad seemed to be an intelligent blighter. He could sense Kusum's frustration. Joseph's mother's maternal adoration submerged her in a cloud of delusion of her son's allure.

The visit was fruitful. They approved her sari-wrapped figure and her submissive silence. Provisional wedding plans were proposed and further meets foreseen. The next visit was with a bunch of relatives to ink the fine print of the dowry and to iron out wedding details. Joseph had barely spoken to her after the initial introductions. The wedding itself was the usual jamboree of fattening food, riotous relatives, and fevered festivities. Both families brought along an entire trove of family and friends. Weddings were rituals of family bonding and occasions to affirm the social pecking order. Cars, clothes, and bejeweled women were flaunted. Future alliances were mooted. The authority of the church as an arbiter of life events was reinforced.

The newlyweds embarked on their honeymoon after the ceremonies concluded. Kusum shuddered at the indignity of it all. Her honeymoon was a hurried harrowing affair. The lakeside hotel room was expensive but seedy. Mosquito hordes and riotous tourists on houseboats deterred any attempts at silent contemplation on the deck outside. The conversation was limited to meal and mating plans. Joseph and Kusum shared no intellectual interests or values. Intimacy was dissociated, hurried, inadequate, and insistent. She was relieved when their stay was over. The disenchantment was mutual. Joseph flew off to Dubai within a week of their wedding. She, like a dutiful daughter-in-law, stayed on with his parents. As the days went by, Kusum felt cheated. Her 'in-laws' had it all worked out. She was more of a caretaker than a wife. Joseph had availed only two weeks' leave from his new job in Dubai constructions. His parents were old and there was no one to look after them. The family had decided that the best solution was to acquire a daughter-in-law. Their own daughter, Joseph's elder sister, stayed just a short drive away. She was busy looking after her husband and her three young children. A daughter-in-law was a cheaper, more reliable, and more economical option for a housekeeper. Kusum's dreams, aspirations, frustrations, and untapped potential had been banned and binned by society and her parents. Kusum was bitter and frustrated

<u>Domesticity:</u>

Kusum was busy from dawn to dusk. She kept the house in order. She ensured that the dogs were fed and that the chicken coop was locked up at night. She had to supervise the servants. Kuttan, the coconut tree climber visited daily, trimming hedges and doing odd jobs. Once a week he brought along his new fanged tree-climbing machine. Coconut trees needed a weekly manicure. Trees had to be climbed every week. Dried fronds were trimmed. Ripe coconuts were felled and sap-sucking beetles spliced open with a sickle. There were always tasks begging to be completed. The pineapple patch was weeded and rat holes filled in. Saprophytic 'ithikkanni' which could swill off a tree's vitality was avulsed and burnt.

Kuttan did innumerable odd jobs around the property. He was enterprising and able. Left to himself he would loiter, loot, and laze. Kuttan's ethics were elastic. His politics, religion, and principles were elastic and tailored to suit his whims. He would sell off half the coconuts if no one watched. The man merited supervision. Yet, like most young Mallu's, Kuttan was versatile and capable of good work. There is always a lot to be done around the property. The boundary wall with its buttress of thorny, flowery Bougainvillea needed attention with periodic trimming and sprucing. A patch of sprouting mushrooms would be gathered and later garnished and curried for a gourmet spread. Ripening pineapples were hooded and festooned in cocoons of their prickly leaves to avert the evil eye and to keep rats away. Soul and sweetness-sucking bushes were weeded out from banana pods.

Kusum was busy. She barely got time to visit her own parents. 'This is your home now' — her mother-in-law would chide her. Her own mother seemed to agree. Joseph, being the son, would inherit his parent's property. Her own parent's house, the one she had grown up in, would one day belong to her brother Kamal. Kamal worked in Bangalore. He loved the city's hustle and bustle. He would sell off the property the day his parents died. Kusum was a wee bit bitter. She had no rancor against Kamal. Patriarchy was tradition. Like many established incoherent practices, patriarchy reflected the agro-economic realities of yesteryear. Practical customs had been enshrined as rent-seeking religious doctrine. The world had changed. Religions were recalcitrant to reform. Male dominance was the unwritten, scrupulously enforced law of the Kerala Syrian Christian community.

She heard the courtyard gate clank. It would be Shankaran the paperman. The newspaperman was always on time. Thomas, her father-in-law was already up. He would be stretched out on his easy chair on the verandah with his legs up on the extended armrests. He would wait for her to fetch the newspaper and to get him his morning tea. Kerala male chauvinism did not allow him to stroll down to the gate to collect the paper. To go to the kitchen and pour out tea for himself was of course, unbecoming, unthinkable, and unnecessary. Thomas was a nice enough chap, thought Kusum. He was friendly and well-read. Yet, having to do chores for him rankled. Kusum had completed her engineering course only a year ago. "If this was all that I was meant to do in life", thought Kusum, "I need not have studied so much". A loud knock snapped Kusum out of her reverie. Mary, the servant, was at the kitchen door. She had brought the newspaper in. The dogs were kenneled and would soon be fed.

Her father-in-law Thomas, looked up and smiled as she brought him his tea, a packet of Marie arrowroot digestive biscuits, and the newspaper. He nodded approvingly. Kusum was a pretty girl. It made sense to acquire a daughter-in-law who was educated. Educated girls were potentially employable. If required, she could pick up a job and supplement the family income. Thomas's wife Shalini had attended school to the 10th grade. Christian girls' schools groomed girls for matrimony and cultured domesticity. Times had changed. Things were different. Girls too, were picking up well-paid jobs. Some of them were better paid than their husbands. Thomas scowled. "He would never let that happen in this household. The man had to be in charge. Women were like family heirlooms. They conducted the household orchestra and were designed to bear babies. He smiled to himself. If Kusum knew what he was thinking, she would be furious. 'Nice tea' he complimented her. Kusum smiled.

Shalini was still in bed. Soon after her son's wedding, her 'rheumatism' had taken a sharp turn for the worse. Formalizing the inevitable, innocuous aches and creaks of age and privileged affluence was the bane of modern medicine and a boon to entitled middle-class women. Shalini retired from household chores after her son's marriage. She stopped contributing to housework. She was generous with advice, forcefully effusive in opinions, and miserly with praise. It was different before Kusum came into the house. Alone with her husband, Shalini had had no option but to be active and well. She handled and supervised housework with energy, viciousness, and vim. She would be up early to oversee household chores. Kusum was the new lady help in the house. Shalini assessed her daughter-in-law's capabilities critically. Kusum was meticulous and able. Shalini handed over the responsibility of daily chores to Kusum. She retained executive power and veto privileges.

Kusum pondered the day's agenda. There was a wedding to be attended today. It was a distant cousin's marriage. Kusum barely knew the family. There would be introductions and appraisals. Weddings were social events. This was when you got to meet all your relatives. A wedding was an arena for status negotiation and focused socializing. This was where you gauged your social standing and affirmed the pecking order of props, perks, and propriety. Weddings were also nuptial bazaars. Older folk kept an eagle eye for potential grooms and brides. Scintillating silhouettes of suitable girls were appraised and approved. Weddings beget more alliances. If you did not attend weddings and funerals, you would miss out on the parish headcount and consequently be wiped out from Saint Peter's register at the pearly gates.

The church ceremony would start at 10 and go on for 3 hours. Weddings and the Sunday church service were conducted in an archaic Syrian script. Most parishioners and many priests did not comprehend the nuances of the incantations. The authoritative incomprehensibility added to the mystique and perversely to the meaning of the service. A church service could drag on for three to four hours depending on how vicious the curate felt. As in most religions, sartorial common sense was sacrificed at the altar of sobriety. Families could not sit together during a church service. Men and women were segregated. Syrian Christian churches appreciated that orthodoxy was the secret of power. The premise was probably true, though Kusum. Orthodoxy, however irrational, enshrined religious authority across the spectrum of religions. Socio-religious reform, like political reform, was a slippery slope fraught with peril.

It was with the assent of the church that the dowry system flourished and was perpetuated. A woman given dowry forfeited her inheritance. The church was reforming, albeit slowly. Reform in religion and politics had to be tailored to the environment. The most catastrophic political consequences occur when functional systems are dismantled without a plan. The Soviet Union collapsed. Reformist Christianity in Europe is being decimated by radical, resurgent organized orthodox Islam. When rigid frameworks are dissolved, the structure and construct of nations and religions crumble and congregational discipline erodes. It was a discipline that ensured that church coffers were overflowing. Religious tenets enshrined male dominance. Males still inherited family property. The church retained power over your purse, property, propriety, and souls. Religion was a potent political force. If you messed with doctrine and ritual, you risked promoting anarchy and atheism.

Kusum was in the kitchen. Today's breakfast would be puttu and plantains. The plantains were from their own courtyard. Kusum watched as Mary filled bamboo cylinders with rice powder. These cylinders would be sealed and then steamed over a brass pot half full of water. A thin topping of coconut kernel added flavor. Mixed and kneaded with plantain and jaggery flakes you had a delectable meal for breakfast. The best cuisine in the world is right here, thought Kusum to herself. Kerala Syrian Christian food was wholesome and healthy. Woke criticism of the Kerala diet as unhealthy was unfounded. Ethnicity and customs reverse-engineered our genomic code. Social class, culture, inheritance, and diet were interlinked. Kerala genes were adapted to coconut oil. Malayalee males had high blood pressure, diabetes, an unfavorable lipid profile, pot bellies, and prickly egos. You could not blame all of this on your diet. Coconut oil was an innocent bystander in a sociocultural genomic avalanche. The oil itself was subject to vicarious infamy.

The doorbell chimed. Kunju, the driver was always on time. Kusum gave him the car keys. Kunju would wipe the windshields, top up the radiator, and check the levels of engine oil and brake fluid. He had been Thomas' driver for ten years now. Kunju used to drive a taxi in his younger days. Now, his eyesight was fading. He could not drive at night or do long-distance trips anymore. Kunju knew his limitations and was reliable. He was the favored driver for three families in the locality. Elderly people did not like to drive. Kerala was short of young working males. Young males wishing to work migrated to other countries where the work ethic was competitive and remunerations respectable. They left their wives at home to care for their parents and property. The families were well off. Ladies needed to go shopping. Kunju had a fixed rate for his services. There was no haggling. Kunju kept busy. He earned enough money to run his house and kitchen in reasonable resourceful splendor. He looked forward to visitors from abroad. Every family had children working overseas. When they came home on leave, they hired his services. There would be a comprehensive list of relations and well-wishers to be visited. Kunju knew the roads and could locate the addresses. The honking incomprehensibility of Indian road customs and the paucity of paved roads and signage deterred expats from driving in Kerala. They paid well for honest courteous service and brought Kuttappan gifts.

The dogs were barking. Mary had not given them breakfast. Where was she? Kusum found her behind the kitchen flirting with Pappan. Pappan was the rubber tapper. On seeing Kusum, Mary quietly withdrew into the kitchen. Pappan picked up his tapping knife, sickle, and bucket and ambled off to work. "Unless you kept an eye on everything, work would grind to a halt", thought Kusum. She had to commit herself to domesticity to consciously exert alert diligent control. Kusum got busy. Breakfast was soon ready. The dogs were fed.

Thomas was reading out obituaries to his wife, Kerala was full of unemployed, unemployable loafers and retired people. Enterprising and hardworking Keralites were overseas or in other states. The retired, the old and the infirm came back to Kerala to die. After their demise, they would, through their kin, exercise their privilege to funereal rites and squabble over choice spots, 'with a view' in the graveyard. Having completed their sojourn from dust to dust in their earthly existence, they would transcend and transform into euphonious wisps of eternity. They would be buried in graveyards their forefathers had built. Kusum was debating with herself. "Did funerals really matter? Did a distinguished funeral really matter to the dead? Was a funeral just an elaborate philosophic pretense to numb the indignity of inconsequence of one's earthly existence?" It was probable that the funeral ceremony and the prayers offered the last sacred rejuvenation of one's soul commencing its journey to a heavenly abode. "Do bonds forged in life tether the spirits of the dead"? Kusum grimaced at her own morbid thoughts. Isolation and the lack of intellectual stimulation were corroding her cognitive edge. She had always considered philosophy to be the last refuge of scoundrels and losers. If she spent six months in this swamp philosophizing, she would be bidding adieu to her aspirations of an academic engineering career.

Kusum was a bright girl. She had always been in the first five in her class. Today, all her friends from the engineering college were in jobs or doing management courses. Here she was, running a kitchen and the courtyard. Joseph, her husband had seemed to be an inconsequential decently decadent chap before the wedding. He too had been revealed as a closet male chauvinistic pig. He had married her and left her to look after his parents and property. She snapped out of her reverie. Thomas was praising her. The food was good and the house was neat. Kusum blushed at this familiar blizzard of accolades as she politely acknowledged the compliments. Housekeeping was not what she wanted to do in life, but as long as she was at it, she would do it well. Complements took the edge off a woman's rancor. Appropriate and tactical complements were tactical barbs in the quiver of tools of males in their facile quest of domestic deigning dominance.

Kusum got back to the old house. Mary was cooking in the kitchen. Cooking was traditional. In earthen pots and over an old brick stove burning dried wood and charcoal. There was a recently acquired gas stove. Cooking gas was however at a premium. Shalini insisted that the servants used firewood. Today, the family would be out for lunch. Dinner would still need to be made. Besides, workers had to be fed and something had to be rustled up for the dogs. Cooking and cleaning were long drawn-out processes. Mary would have the house to herself. Kusum had the gnawing angst that Pappan would be back from the plantation to keep her company. Lower classes and the aristocracy were at the liberated poles of the morality spectrum. Both cohorts were insulated from the decadence-dampening middle-class hypocrisy that masqueraded as virtue.

The old and the new wings of their house were independent. The ancestral house was in a classical Kerala architectural pattern and had its traditional kitchen. This was where the daily cooking went on. The new wing had been added on for convenience and perceived style. It also served as a statement of affluence and of contemporary solvency. A twin-wing design had its plusses. They could lock up the new building when they went out. The old kitchen, dining area, and two old bedrooms would be open for Mary to clean, cavort, and work in.

<u>The Loft:</u>

The loft above the old building was a sanctum where Mary would not venture alone. Shalini did not have the curiosity or vim to expend energy in any exploration. Thomas was too laid back and lazy for physical labor. Kusum surmised that there would have been a time when the loft functioned as a store room. The loft could still be used. The lighting was however poor and other storage spaces were available. A solid wooden ladder led up to the loft. There were storerooms outside the main house now. Coconuts were stored in a shed in the courtyard. These would be sold to wholesale merchants from town who would roll by in their mini trucks. In another shed was a press. This was where the rubber sap was molded into sheets. These sheets would be cut and later sold to factories in town. These rubber factories made myriad products from flip-flops to rubber mats. The loft was sparingly used. A few banana bunches and the occasional basket of mangos would still be ensconced in the loft for ripening by Kuttan.

It was time to get ready for the wedding. Shalini had dressed up and had finished her make-up. She had a cupboard full of silk sarees. Choosing the right one for each occasion was arduous and often stressful. Shalini frowned as a disheveled Kusum emerged from the kitchen. Scarcely concealing her irritation, she told Kusum to hurry up and get ready. Kusum would wear a new saree for the occasion. As a recent bride, she would be subject to scrutiny. She chose a pink silk saree. This had been gifted to her by Thomas. He would appreciate it. Kuttappan brought the car from the garage and was waiting outside. He was in wedding party mode, in a clean white dhoti and shirt. Traditionally and by convention, drivers of the entourage were also invited to wedding lunches. They would sit at one of the corner tables and would be served the same food as the other guests. Wedding lunches were elaborate affairs. Food would be served on Banana leaves. There would be rice and dal and aviyal (a vegetable mish mash), an assortment of vegetable curries, pickles, papad, fish, and a meat dish. This would be topped off with a Payasam (a rice-based sweet porridge). Drivers had hearty appetites and would have second or third helpings. Folks like Kusum would nibble at the various delicacies and still manage to feel stuffed.

Kunju honked. The car was ready on the porch. They traipsed in. It was an hour's drive to church. They reached the state highway. Despite its presumptuous name, this highway was a narrow potholed affair where buses and trucks jostled with cows and pedestrians. The flow of traffic was regulated by muscle, common sense, and convictions rather than by formalized traffic rules. The car left the main road now. Soon they were bumping along a mud track. Kusum sat in the back with Shalini. Joseph sat in front of the driver. The car was an Ambassador, an Indianized minimalistic version from the erstwhile Morris garages. This old car was spacious and sturdy. It was low on technology and a bit of a fuel guzzler. The ambassador was, in its heyday, the most popular car in Kerala. It was equipped for bad roads. The Ambassador's Izuzi engine was powerful. The car was not saddled with too many gadgets. The technology permitted a capable driver or a roadside mechanic to maintain and repair it with a set of spanners and an attitude. Kusum's dad had an imported Honda. A Honda was smooth and comfortable to drive on a well-maintained freeway. There were no manicured roads around Kottayam. These cars were not meant for the mud tracks of rural Kerala. Kusum looked out of the car window. The view was rustically scenic. The road meandered along the riverside with its fishermen and the odd dhobi. There was a gentle curve of the road. A hill loomed ahead. The church was halfway up the hill. The rains were yet to wreak havoc and the road was negotiable.

There were other cars ahead of them heading for the same festivities. Following their car was a bus hired by the bride's family. A white luxury car frilled with flowers honked past. They glimpsed the demure bride inside, flanked by her mother and a stern-looking aunt. The bride was from another town. The church soon came into view. The wedding hall by the church was festooned and enlivened with ribbons and balloons. Kunju dropped them off at the church entrance. The function would be starting in a short while. Kusum and Shalini found a place for themselves in one of the front pews. Thankachan would debate church and party politics with other elders outside. The incantations started. There would be an hour of various prayers and songs before the actual wedding ceremony.

Christians in Kerala had adapted many Hindu customs to their repertoire of customs. One of these rituals was the tying of a Managalsutra around the Bride's neck. The Christian Managalasutra was called a Minnu. A cross on the minnu was the only inkling of Christian religious antecedents. The Minnu was blessed by the vicar. The thread that would secure the minnu around the bride's neck would later be replaced by a gold chain. Traditionalists insisted that the minnu reflected the sanctity of marriage. Women were extolled to ensure that their minnu never came off. In church, as part of the rites, the groom had to tie the knot of possession. Any fumbling in front of the eagle-eyed congregation would occasion ridicule. Young men often practiced knot tying in private so that they would not fumble during the ceremony. Today's bride was a graduate of one of the local colleges. The boy was an engineer in the gulf. The dowry was ten lakhs. Twenty thousand went to the church. Another fifty thousand would have been spent on the wedding lunch. Most of the remaining money would be used for the boy's sister's dowry. It was a familiar sequence. The church was the only net beneficiary.

The wedding ceremony was over. The registry was signed by the couple. Lunch was well cooked. Wedding cooking was done on the premises. This ensured that the Food was warm and palatable. With the couple seated on the dais and after the priests blessed the food, lunch started. Kusum looked around. She often marvelled at the quantity of rice a Keralite could consume. It was not surprising that Kerala was the 'Diabetic Capital' of India. Kusum watched in awe as mountains of rice were systematically demolished by people at her table. Everyone ate with their hands. Some guests would roll rice into a tight ball before tossing it into their mouths. A few, like Kusum who had been brought up outside Kerala ate quaintly, with some loss of efficiency using only their fingertips. It would be futile, foolish, and pretentious to ask for a spoon. Someone would pass a rude comment and Thomas would be embarrassed. After lunch, they queued up to wash their hands. Kunju had finished lunch too and was burping loudly. He had loosened the Mundu around his waist during lunch, to let his stomach expand. He now retired the Mundu with an expert hand.

A heavy meal of rice is intensely soporific. They were all drowsy during the drive back. Thomas was nodding off in the car. As soon as they reached home, he paid Kunju, went straight to his room, and slept. Kusum had to let Mary off. Household chores were over. Clothes had been washed and strung up outside to dry. Dogs had been fed. Pappan would be given tea and his daily wages at five in the evening. Kusum decided that she would rest for a while. She had changed out of her silk saree into a more comfortable salwar. She lay on the bed in the old room and shut her eyes. She could hear a rat scrabbling in the loft above. She would get Pappan to check out the loft and position a trap. Rats could wreak havoc in the store.

The Chathans

Kusum slept. She woke up with a start. There was some ruckus going on in the loft above. Kususm glanced at the clock. It was four thirty. It would be another thirty minutes before Pappan came in from the plantation. She listened to the sounds coming from the loft. It sounded as if a box of sorts was being dragged across the floor. Kusum had a sudden attack of panic. Could it be that robbers had sneaked up into the loft? She jumped out of bed ready to scoot outside and raise an alarm. Kusum checked herself. It would be highly improbable that robbers would be after anything in the loft. There were sacks of potatoes jars of condiments there and a few bunches of bananas hanging from a rope tied to the ceiling. The only thing of possible value in the loft was an old antique box. This box was locked. There was no key available. She had discovered the box a couple of weeks ago when she had gone up to the loft with Mary and Pappan. Kusum had asked Thomas about it. "That was a box which belonged to my grandfather. It has been locked for as long as I can remember. There must be some property deeds or other documents inside. Whatever is inside the box would be of no use today". Thomas had continued. "We cannot open the box without breaking the lock and cracking the lid. When you set up a house and want an antique piece for décor, you could get it opened and polished." The box was of solid teak wood. It would one day make an exquisite decorative piece.

The scraping sounds from the loft continued. Kusum was now convinced that someone was moving the box. She gathered up her courage and decided to explore. If she ran to her in-laws they would laugh at her. There was no light in the loft. Though it was early evening, the inside of the loft would be dusky, dark, dank, and dusty. She picked up an emergency lamp and climbed up the ladder. The loft door swung open as she pushed. Holding the light in front of her, she climbed in. The shelves with food articles were as she remembered them. There was no sign of any damage caused by rats. Two bunches of plantains had been hung from the ceiling by Pappen to ripen. One of them was swinging softly. She went closer. A ripe plantain had been plucked from the bunch. Could it have been a rat? There was a disc on the rope suspending the plantains. This would prevent a rat from climbing down from the ceiling to the plantains. There was stool below the plantain bunch that she had not seen before. Kusum guessed that a child could climb on the stool to reach the bunch. Kusum moved the stool out of the way and walked deeper into the loft. She saw the box. It was lying in the center of the loft away from the wall. There were marks as if someone had dragged the box from its place near the wall. On either side of the box, there were small footprints in the dust. These were human footprints, but small. They could have easily been those of a child.

Kusum flashed her torch into the corner of the loft. There lay a banana peel. Rats did not peel bananas. Kusum felt a tingle of excitement. Surprisingly, she had no perceptible fear. Kusum abruptly froze. Did she hear a giggle coming from the corner? She slowly backed out of the loft. Climbing down the ladder she closed the loft door softly behind her. The clock was chiming. It was five PM. She would need to make tea for Pappan and for her in-laws. Kusum went to the kitchen. Pappan had come back and was stacking some firewood he had brought back from the plantations. As she gave him tea and biscuits, she was tempted to ask him to climb into the loft and investigate. Something restrained her. This was her secret. She would check it out herself. Pappan left with his daily wages. He would keep fifty rupees for his toddy and give the rest of the money to his wife to run the house.

Toddy shops in Kerala ran a brisk business. There were regulars like Pappan who toiled through the day. The money they earned, kept toddy owners in business. There were excise duties and bribes to be paid. But overall, the toddy business was lucrative. Kusum did not grudge Pappan his toddy. After a day of back-breaking work in the scorching sun and baked fields, a man needed some relaxation. Kusum sat out on the porch with Shalini and Thomas as she evolved a strategy. She decided against sharing her secret with Thomas and Shalini. Kusum was sure that the key to the puzzle lay locked up in the box. The key was missing. She felt more intrigue than fear. Her cheeks flushed with excitement, and Kusum evolved a plan. The mystery of the loft evoked intense anticipation and a heightened sense of adventure. She decided against asking Thomas anything about the loft or the box. Thomas was perceptive and would sense connections and scout the intrigue. He might decide to get the box down and break it open. It was best to keep him out of the loop.

The box in the loft and its secret were hers to unravel and to acquire. Meanwhile, it was getting darker. On Thomas's cue, they shifted their chairs outside to the courtyard. There was a raised perimeter of coarse-grained white sand all around the house. This was tradition and like many traditions was moored in practicality. A swathe of coarse sand was an ingenious Kerala way of keeping snakes away from the house. Snakes avoided the loose sand. It slowed them down and took away their stealth. If a snake did venture out on the sand chasing a frog or a chick, you would hear it slithering around. Hearing the rustle in your yard could avoid the snake or chase it away. The simple expedient of stomping hard where you stood would coax most snakes to make a detour. Snakes perceived vibrations conducted along the ground and would keep their distance. Snakes had little fear. They would not get into altercations with humans unless they were cornered. It made no sense to kill snakes. They kept the rat population in check. The sand perimeter was a boon during monsoons. There were no mud puddles around the house. You could walk around the house without getting your feet filthy.

They switched off the house lights. It was a familiar ritual now. With the house lights off, they could see the stars as they peeked out one by one. There was peace in the darkness occasionally interrupted by the chirp of crickets. The moon would rise later that night. They watched mesmerized as each star ventured out of the shroud of darkness. Thomas had explained to Kusum how to discern stars from planets. Planets did not twinkle like the stars. Kusum closed her eyes and made a wish as she glimpsed a shooting star. There were plenty of shooting stars tonight. Rocks from the asteroid belt or space debris would feel the thrall of Earth's gravity. They would then be incinerated in a fiery descent and burn up before they reached the earth's surface. Meteors streaking across the dark sky into oblivion were spectacular. Only a few of the small ones made it to the earth's surface. Large meteors, which are fortunately rare, create craters when they strike the ground. A huge meteorite heralded the ice age and caused the extinction of dinosaurs. Debris from the crater of collision raised a dust cloud. This reflective cloud blotted out sunlight for so long that the earth cooled. The resulting ice age froze the dinosaurs to extinction. Kusum pondered if a man-made cloud could reverse global warming. Messing with the forces of nature was potentially hazardous. She could see man-made satellites moving slowly across the sky. There were military satellites, weather satellites, and communication satellites. Someone somewhere was watching our every move. 'I wonder if they could see me if I waved". Kusum killed the thought. The future of engineering was stratospheric. Kusum wondered if a 'spray of low-cost satellites could link us to the stars or at least provide reliable resilient communication. In the distance she could see the lights of a commercial airplane, too high for its sound to be heard, inching across the sky.

A formation of bats flew majestically overhead. Bats are nocturnal marauders. There was a banyan tree in the temple where they slept during the day. You saw them, hanging upside down from the branches like some overgrown fruit. At night they flew off to the lush hills, where they would feast on fruit. Bats were the subject of lore. They were also unique biological specimens. They are the only mammals who fly. Indeed, they are nimbler fliers than many birds. Kusum had seen the charred body of one of the bats, electrocuted while flying near a high-voltage cable. It was as big as a house cat with a wizened humanoid face and leathery wings. The wings were like parchment and when spread out could measure a good four feet across. Bats navigate using ultrasound waves. These are reflected back to them off obstacles.

Small bats which were a different subspecies. One night, a small bat had flown into their house by mistake. Trapped inside the four walls it had flown, from room to room at a furious pace. A bat's capacity to avoid obstacles while flying at high speed is phenomenal. In the future, nimble autonomous military aircraft powered with AI would potentially emulate these bats. The bat had finally escaped through a window. Some small bats were carnivorous. The vampire bat, popularized in Dracula Lore was known to be a bloodsucker. The larger bats subsisted on fruit. "At least I hope so," thought Kusum. If they turned carnivorous and descended in a flock to attack, they would be deadly.

It was dark. Kusum and Shalini went into the house. The lights came on. Food was warmed. The spectacular night sky dulled as the house lit up. They shared a light dinner of rice, fish curry, and 'thorns' a Syrian Christian specialty of vegetable and coconut mish mashes. A light breeze barely ruffled the leaves of the mango tree outside the dining room. Kusum warmed up meat broth and rice for the dogs. She fed the dogs and let them loose. They ran barking around the courtyard pausing to check out familiar and unfamiliar odors. A rat raced down its scoot hole, with the dogs digging furiously and futilely behind. A few birds snapped out of dreamy reveries to rise into the air before settling down again. The dogs completed their fury patrol. They would now come back, puffed and panting, to guard the house.

The family slept in the new building. The old house was locked from the outside. Thomas and Shalini were early sleepers. They were in bed by nine. The house was eerily quiet now. Kusum heard the dogs bark as they chased a vagrant bandicoot down its burrow. Dog's ears bristle with sounds we do not hear. Different animals perceive and process sensory phenomena differently. Humans and cats are dominantly visual creatures. Dogs have intense hearing and an acute sense of smell. They hear the roll of wheels of the devil's chariot and smell brewing trouble. On full moon nights when the spirits traipsed a rhapsody, a dog somewhere would yodel in consternation. His wail would be taken up by the others in an eerie mystic ritual of defiance and denial.

Thomas' grandfather was Chackochan, a lawyer. He was a scholar, philosopher, magician, and mystic. He was from an era when knowledge and wisdom were untethered and unencumbered by protocols and mechanistic evidence bases. He was a wise man who understood the language of animals and could fathom and gauge the moods of Mother

Earth. Kusum heard many stories about him. He was respected by all for his erudition and feared by many for his uncanny ability to implement justice. Unscrupulous businessmen and tyrannical landlords fled on hearing his tread. There was a Robin Hood aura around Chackochan's name. His spirit and soul transcended the dusty dominion of material molecular life and existence. Kusum could sense his influence and aura in the recesses of the old house. The loft transcended time zones and the creaky ladder to the loft seemed to proffer a gateway to Chackochans life and realm. Kusum remembered the box and the sounds she had heard in the loft. The little footprints and the banana peel in the loft would have, thought Kusum, some glib, unglamorous, woke, and logical explanation. "It must have been rats", she told herself. "A brew of boredom and a fertile imagination could be hallucinogenic".

She doused the room lights and put on her reading lamp. Down the corridor, she could hear Thomas snore. She picked up a novel from the bookshelf. She would read herself to sleep. Kusum's thoughts kept drifting back to the locked box in the loft. She decided that she had to check it out. She got out of bed and pulled on her jeans. There was a flashlight in her room. She picked it up and tiptoed out of the house, locking the front door behind her. The dogs came up sniffing and wagging their tails. Disappointed that she did not want to play with them, they returned to their bandicoot hunts. The old house was dark. She opened the door without putting the lights on. She did not want to disturb and perturb Thomas and Shalini.

Using her flashlight she climbed the ladder to the loft and unfastened the latch door. She had to keep the flashlight down and use both hands to push the loft door open. As the hatch creaked open she could hear a scurry and patter of little feet from the loft. Startled, she dropped her flashlight. There was a light in the loft coming from around the corner. Gaining all the courage she clambered into the loft. Ahead of her, the trunk lay open. There was a small lantern by its side. Kusum picked up the lantern and looked inside the box. Inside the box, there were stacks of old books. Some of the books were in English, but most of them seemed to be in Malayalam. Kusum could barely read Malayalam. She recognized the names of some authors. They were prominent literary figures of a bygone era. Did she hear a whisper in the dark? She paused and looked around.

Kusum had an eerie feeling that she was being watched. She turned her attention back to the trunk. At the bottom of the trunk, beneath the pile of books was a small jewel box covered in red leather embossed with a gold inscription. As she picked the box up out of the container, she heard agitated whispers from the corner of the loft. She pried the lid of the box open with her nail. Inside the box was a small black book. On top of the book was a thin silver chain with an exquisitely carved pendant. She slipped the chain around her neck, picked up the book, and kept the box back. There was a babble of voices from the corner. As Kusum watched enthralled, a little man stepped out of the darkness. He was about a foot tall and had a small dhoti around his waist. In his hand was a small stick. His face looked wizened, his hair was jet black and his skin gleamed as though polished with some exotic oil. His eyes were sad and wise.

As Kusum stood frozen, more such men stepped out of the darkness. They were all similarly attired and each carried a little stick. As the little men seemed to show no inclination to hurt her, Kusum relaxed. The first man was speaking now. "Please don't take the book out of the box", his voice was imploring. "If some evil one gets it, they will make us slaves again". The man looked so agitated that Kusum immediately put the book back in its box. She started removing the necklace from around her neck, but the man stopped her. "You wear the chain. It is for you. Don't take it off. Not even when you are bathing. If you need to call us at any time, just rub the pennant". "Who are you?" Kusum finally found her voice. The man had taken the book with its leather-bound box and replaced it inside the trunk. He shut the trunk. Taking out a golden key from a fold in his dhoti. He locked it. "Sit," he told Kusum pointing to the box. "Let me tell you a story". Two of the little men had wiped the top of the box clean. Kusum obediently sat down.

The man who had spoken to her was obviously their chief. He stood facing her while the others formed a semicircle behind him. "My name is Tinku" said the little man proudly. "We are Kuttichathans". Tinku paused. Kusum was aware of the history and the folklore of Kerala. She remembered the legend of the Chathans. These little imps were created as God's helpers. Some misdeeds got them banished from heaven. They had endless energy and a penchant for mischief. "Chackochan was our friend", the little man continued. The necklace you are wearing now is the one we gave him. Chackochan told us about you. We recognized you the day you came into the house". This was implausible. Kusum and the ancestor in question were separated by three generations. Kusum had never met any elder in her husband's family before her marriage fixture. Chackochan had died a hundred years before Kusum was born. It all seemed a little far-fetched. Considering the events of the enchanted evening, however, Kusum kept an open mind. She believed what the man said and she sensed its cosmic resonance. "The black book has all the magical chants which can control us," said Tinku. "If it falls into the wrong hands, we will be enslaved again". Kusum raised an eyebrow quizzically. "We were slaves, before Chakochan rescued us from the Kutothram Pillai", piped up another Kuttichathan. One of the kuttichathans came forward and parted his hair. Kusum could see a small puncture hole. "This is where Kutothram Pillai drove nails into our heads. Any Chathan with a magic nail in his head became a slave. He would obey anything his master commanded". A snippet from a technology uptake flashed through Kusum's Brain. An entrepreneur engineering genius was designing Brain Implants for cognitive augmentation. Brain control was the unsaid imponderable. Kusum subconsciously patted her own head. She could feel no implant. She smiled at her own irrational insecurity.

Kusum was tired. She suppressed a yawn. She wondered what time it was. She was not wearing her watch. Tinku seemed to read her mind. He dipped his hand into a fold in his dhoti and brought out a watch with a silver chain. "It will be midnight soon. I think you should go and sleep. Tomorrow night, we will meet again", said Tinku. Kusum was not going to be hustled out. "And what are you guys going to do", she asked them. "We sleep during the day, at least most of us do", said another Kuttichathan, casting a sly glance at Tinku. Tinku looked stern. "We have a lot of odd jobs to do with our magic. We read these books, whenever we are free". "What were you doing with the trunk in the afternoon?" asked Kusum. The Kuttichathan looked sheepish. It was my turn to cook and I wanted a recipe book. Kusum did not remember seeing any recipe book in the trunk.

The Kuttichathan saw the look of confusion on her face and continued. We have a withdrawal facility. He looked at Kusum with the air of a conjurer. "Think about any book you want to read". Kusum wondered what she should ask for. There was a book on nuclear physics that had not been available in the college library. It was written by a Nobel Laurette. An Indian Edition had not been forthcoming. The international version was too expensive for her to buy. She had wanted to refer to it. Before she could say anything, Tinku opened the box again. Before her startled eyes, he put in his hand and pulled out a glossy brand-new book. He handed it over to Kusum. "Read it", he told her. When you have finished reading it, you can choose another book. He closed the trunk again.

Kusum gingerly picked up the book. The book was brand new, glistening with pixie dust, and seemed to intuitively assist Herb as she sought the index and scrolled the contents. still warm from the press. It was the latest edition and was literally warm from the press.

Kusum closed the book with a wink of thanks to Tinku. She would have to smuggle the book into her room. "Good night", she told the Kuttichanthans and left. Tinku brought the lantern along, to help her get down from the loft. He picked up her flashlight and gave it to her. Kusum tiptoed out, locking the old house behind her. The dogs looked up, wagging their tails as if sharing a secret with her. This was reassuring. The dogs did not sense anything evil in these little men. She opened the front door and wafted in. Thomas's snores had changed in tenor and notched a higher volume. Kusum went into her bedroom and closed the door. After hiding the book on her shelf, she snuggled under a sheet and closed her eyes. In a few minutes, she was fast asleep.

She dreamt of Kuttichathans. There was a grand party she was presiding over. She sat at the head of a long table with rows of Kuttichathans in high chairs on both sides. Food would appear on their plates by magic, course after course. When you desired a dish, you did not have to ask. You just had to think about it. There was music from an unseen band in the backyard. At the end of dinner, Tinku, seated on her right held up his goblet of wine. "To Kusum", he proposed a toast with a twinkle in his eye. The other Kuttichathans had started chanting now, "Kusum, Kusum, Kusum". The sound was getting louder and louder and more intolerable. She closed her ears and opened her eyes. "Kusum, Kusum", it was Shalini. It is six in the morning and your alarm has been ringing for some time. She sat up groggily. The day had to start. She wondered if the entire episode had been a dream. She put her hand around her neck and felt the silver chain. She looked at the bookshelf. There it was, 'Nuclear Physics by Anderson'. It had not all been a dream after all. Maybe it was. Kusum realized she had straddled the chasm to an alternative universe. Dreams here had substance and earthy reality was ethereal. She got out of bed and was ready for her daily chores.

She opened the front door and headed for the old house. Everything was as she had left it the evening before. She got out milk from the refrigerator and kept it on the stove. Damn, she had forgotten the lighter. She would have to go all the way back to the new house. She heard a sound next to her. There was a smiling Kuttichathan standing there with a lighter in his hand. "Thanks", said Kusum, looking around. It would be chaotic if the maid or Shalini sauntered in. The chathan read her mind. "Don't worry, they are sleeping We have locked up the dogs for you". Kusum smiled in gratitude. She had a feeling that life was going to be easier for her from now. There was also a nasty foreboding that matters could get complicated. She was right on both counts.

Mary was impressed when she came in. The kitchen looked transformed. Mary always considered Kusum quite a novice at home management. Today everything in the kitchen was spick and span. The dogs had been locked in. Milk had not boiled over. Kusum finished off her day's chores early and settled with her book. Thomas was surprised and pleased with his daughter-in-law's efficient, ebullient, enthusiasm. "Where did you get this book", he asked her seeing the brand-new edition Kusum was reading. "It was in the trunk", she replied. She had not lied, she thought to herself. She had not specified which trunk it had come from. There were no plans for the day. Thomas too had settled with a PG Wodehouse. He had a large collection of books. There are three cohorts of the literate, thought Kusum. There were those who read in a quest to learn. Reading allowed them to open their minds to implement new visions and ideals. There were those who just read for the joy of reading. Then, there were those whose intellect was so severely constrained by the demands of life, that they did not read books at all. Thomas was of the second strata. He read for the joy of reading.

Thomas had been a bank officer in his time. Every month, after payday, he would buy a book or two from 'DCM Books', the best bookstall in town. He chose his books seemingly at random after prowling the aisles and perusing the shelves for an hour. There was a method in his madness. His book choices straddled every realm from philosophy to satire, science, and art. He nursed and nurtured this habit over decades. He now had a formidable personal library. His wife did not appreciate or share his literary passions. Shalini had taken the car and gone shopping. This was her favorite pastime. Shalini prided herself on getting the best bargains. She would spend a thousand rupees on the driver and on petrol to save a hundred rupees at a seasonal sale. Woke philosophy and weak economic rationale allowed her to exult and indulge in her own concept of market wisdom. Shalini was one of the unsung heroes of new economic theories which would roil ruinous political discourse over the next few decades.

Kottayam town was ten kilometers away. The road was in poor repair and the drive would take an hour. Shalini would be back from her shopping by around two in the afternoon. After a short gloat over the loot, she would be ready for lunch. Kusum and Thomas decided that they would wait for her. Kusum was hungry. She decided to fix herself and Thomas a little snack. Mary was busy doing the laundry. Kusum walked into the kitchen and almost bumped into a kuttichathan. He had a tray in his hand with two cups of tea and a few cookies. He winked at her and gave her the tray. Kusum looked around hurriedly with concern. She was wee bit worried about the sporadic assistive chathanic enthusiasm. She looked askance in consternation to see if Mary or Pappen had spotted him. The little man winked. "Don't worry" said the Kuttichathan. "We know how to stay out of sight. You see, we have been around incognito for a long time". Kusum looked around in consternation. When she turned back, the little man had disappeared. After tea, Kusum retired to her room with her new book.

The book on nuclear physics was scintillating. There is a special joy in reading the work of someone who thinks and conceptualizes beyond and outside the constrictive envelope of conventional academic rigor. Kusum enjoyed reading. Fundamental concepts and original thought fascinated her. She had been a keen student and it was easy to rekindle her learning genes. Learning involves the assimilation of selected information. The structure and skeleton sculpted by primary education were permissive and facilitative, paving the way to further learning and to the endless quest for enlightenment. Knowledge involves application and fine-tuning of learned skills. Wisdom was awareness of the limits of knowledge and the key to fulfillment. Appreciation, Accolades, and a decent livelihood were incidentals for the truly accomplished. Kusum had not chosen pure science for her majors because of disillusionment with the academic content of the courses available and a disdain for the rote-based approach to learning.

While the structure was vital to the creation of educational edifices, the resultant hierarchy stifled thoughts and ideas. The existing scientific system was adept at the preservation of privilege by snuffing out originality. Individual brilliance was seldom sustainable in science research. Financial, computing, and infrastructural needs for the validation of concepts were daunting. True research was impossible outside structured establishments. The ones who managed to make a mark in institutes were those who had few ideas but were blessed with dogged resilient endurance. Many great brains were wasted and myriad brilliant ideas were binned. Method rather than the Mad strokes of genius would always be preferred preference and acceptance. Conformational coherence was key to academic accolades. Conventional concepts of originality were constrained and hypocritical, thought Kusum. She was daydreaming again. Kusum snapped out of her reverie. The book had ignited dormant desires for self-actualization. Kusum glowed with confidence in the aura of a mystical concordance she could fathom but not define. She knew she would leave her footprints on the sands of time.

Back from her reverie, Kusum wondered how she would ever make her dreams come true. The humdrum of domesticity could numb ambition. Kitchen fires were sustained by the flickering embers of women's unfulfilled potential. Kerala could be a dead end for ambitious women. Kusum knew that she could not chisel her skills or nurture a reputation in Kerala. There were few institutes of excellence that had not been kidnapped by the expedience of vested interests of religious or business groups or by politicians. Publications and peer interaction were key to intellectual fruition. Kusum weighed the odds. She had a few factors in her favor. It was fortunate that Thomas was a closet intellectual. He would understand her angst and tacitly condone her clandestine endeavors. Kusum swore that she would not remain a homemaker forever. She had time and she had the chathans to support her. With the chathan's help she would have access to books and to research material. Kusum shimmered with excitement. She would forge her own future. Kusum started reading in earnest. She made notes. Thomas snoozed in his armchair with an open book on his bare chest. A gentle breeze tickled the mango tree in the courtyard sending its leaves into rustling raptures. Kusum kept reading. After a couple of hours, they heard the car honk. The car docked on the porch. Shalini was back. Kuttappan helped her to carry up the purchases of the day. The tea tray had been cleared. Her little friends kept themselves busy. Lunch was steaming hot and delectable. Shalini was impressed. Afterward, the tables were cleared and plates were washed. It was siesta time. Kuttappan and Mary left. Kusum decided to rest in the afternoon. She went to her room and slept. Tonight, she would visit the loft again.

Kusum woke up feeling someone poking her cheek. She opened her eyes. A kuttichathan was by her bed. "We made tea and pakodas. You can take it from the kitchen", It was past five. She found the tea and snacks ready on the kitchen table. She gave Pappan his tea, refreshments, and his wages. She then carried the tray to the verandah. Thomas was already up. His eyes lit up when he saw the pakodas. He picked one up and nibbled it. The pakodas were simply perfect in taste and texture. With a grunt of appreciation, he gobbled up a couple. Shalini soon joined them on the verandah. They sat in silence, watching the stars emerge one by one. There was a letter for her from Joseph. Shalini had picked it up at the post office on her way back from town. He had sent letters to her and to his parents. He was doing well in his job and was likely to be made a manager soon. He would not get leave for a year. There was no suggestion that Kusum should join him. Kusum suppressed the tinge of irritation she felt. She was being taken for granted. She looked at the sky. A fiery meteorite curved an audacious incendiary arc above their heads. Kusum closed her eyes and then smiled. She would prove herself against all odds. Somewhere in the dark, a gecko chirped his assent.

Thomas was in an animated exposition of Kerala polity. The conversation soon drifted to Kerala's evolution and history. The princely states of Trivandrum and Kochi and the presidency of Malabar forged their own unique cultures and character. Thomas had an excellent fund of general knowledge. It was intensely educational listening to him. Thomas had seen Kerala evolving from the era of the British Raj to the cacophonous dysfunctional democracy it is today. There was incremental but absolute social progress. Many unjust conventions and practices had been annulled. Bonded labor, had been prevalent in Kerala a couple of generations ago. Whole families of servants used to belong to a particular family. Nehruvian socialism and roaring red Marxism had done a lot for the emancipation of these people. Tragically, the political scramble for populism had led to a race to the bottom. There were no winners in today's 'Game of Thrones' except the privileged political class and a raucously opinionated press. The philosophy of all political parties had been hijacked by special interest groups. There was hardly any industrial investment in Kerala because of unruly political goons. The vicarious prosperity of acquisitive redistribution led to a stagnant stalemate of growth and development. Social Liberation and scientific education had to go hand in hand, thought Kusum. You could not have emancipation based on envy, distrust, class, and caste divides. There had to be a simultaneous inculcation of a value system. Kusum was aware that Thomas was a closet Marxist and a rebel at heart. The church however frowned at left-wing political philosophy and its atheistic underpinning. Thomas was careful to keep his feelings to himself. He had terminated his discourse. They remained in silent rumination watching the stars. Shalini was getting hypoglycemic and restless. Soon it was dinner time.

Kusum went in to warm the food. Her little friends had already done the job for her. She sat in the kitchen, glancing at the newspaper headlines while they set and laid out the table. Thomas and Shalini trooped in. Dinner was a big hit. "Kusum has become a great cook", Shalini commented. Thomas looked at her questioningly, mildly suspicious but unsure of what to say. Kusum smiled to herself. Kuttichathans, for all their mischievous reputation, was great house help. After dinner, Thomas and Shalini turned in for the night. Kusum got back to her astrophysics book.

Taking a break, she examined the necklace she was wearing. It was distinctive and pretty. Only she could sense the power that flowed through it. Kusum had worn and concealed the necklace inside her blouse top. No one had noticed it during the day. She realized that she would have to concoct a story about the necklace. The story about it would need to be ready, the next time she went out in a sari. It was well-nigh impossible to conceal anything in a sari-blouse ensemble. She examined the pendant. After so many years in the box, it had not lost its gleam. She rubbed it between her finger and thumb. There was a little bustle behind her. There was Tinku. He gave her a cute little bow. He snapped his fingers. Another kuttichathan appeared with a tray in his hand. There was a glass of juice for her and some tapioca chips. Kusum padded across and locked her bedroom door. If Shalini peeped in, it would be difficult to explain away the midnight snack even if the Kuttichathans themselves disappeared. "Tell me more about yourself", said Kusum keeping her feet on the bed. Tinku plonked himself near her feet and started his tale.

"Let me start off here by saying that we have been around for a long, long time. We saw the dinosaurs in all their majesty. We shivered with them in the ice age when the cloud of dust from a meteorite impact blotted out the sun for months. We saw homo sapiens overcome their stronger and more intelligent Neanderthal cousins". said Tuttu. "We were created by the Gods, to battle evil. We did our jobs well. We do not have the privilege you earthly beings have, of growing old and dying. Our work too is never-ending, for there is no end to evil. When the Gods alone controlled us, we were happy. But then, some of us were impatient". Tintu looked accusingly at a little wiry chathan who was looking very sheepish. We kept pestering the gods for more work, more tasks. The Gods got incensed. They gave us freedom. We were granted semi-autonomy. Some powerful sorcerers and magicians started using us for their purposes. Some of the errands were harmless. More often, they used us and our power to create mischief".

"Your husband's great grandfather Chackochan, was a great man. He devoted his life to the battle against evil. Some evil powers tried to use us against him. That was their mistake. We were created as God's helpers. Saints and great men straddle the realm between heaven and earth and between man and God. We will never harm them. Chackochan realized that we were being exploited. He took us under his wing. Liberating us from the clutches of sorcerers was not easy. Chackochan had to toil for thirty years to crack the sorcerer's codes. The secret spells he used to free us from the sorcerers is in his diary. That is the book you saw in the box in the loft. We guard that box with our lives. If anyone were to get the book, they could undo all that Chackochan did. They could make us slaves again".

Kusum was looking sleepy by now and her eyelids were drooping. As she suppressed a yawn, Tinku smiled. "Go to sleep now. You are our new guardian", he told her.

"Chackochan warned us to be vigilant. The sorcerers get impatient. They try their best to get us back under their wing. We have great powers. But God never gave us free will. Humans have this gift. We need a human to lead us into battle. Nature is with us. So are the kings of the forest and the queens of the rivers. We will all unite and work in harmony against black magic and sorcery. Chackochan said that a blue-eyed girl would come into the house. She would lead and protect us. We knew it was you, the day you stepped in". Kusum yawned again. Tinku stood aside as Kusum changed and got ready for bed. She climbed into bed. Tinku put out the lights and tucked Kusum in. She was exhausted. Sleep came easily. One of the chathans curled up on a sofa in her room. Kusum was under their protection.

In the early hours of the morning, she started dreaming again. She was at the head of a long dining table in a wooden hall. Rows of Kuttichathans sat on either side, all digging into their dinners. Suddenly there was a loud knock on the door. The Chathans looked around, they were looking at her and waiting for her to respond. The click of spoons and forks ceased. The knocking continued. She groggily opened her eyes. She was in her bedroom again and the knock was from the door. She could hear Shalini's voice. "Kusum, Kusum, it is six 'O' clock". She got up. Another day had begun.

Kusum learns Magic:

Kusum shuddered as she reminisced about the day's adventure. If the chathans had not helped her Chandy would have broken her and made her his plaything. Both Chandy and she were back in civilization now. Kusum could not get justice for the assault or protection from Chandy without full disclosure of an enigma she could not fathom. Kusum wondered how she would face Chandy. She decided against telling Thomas anything. The dimensions and domain of her battle were beyond the realm of rational human comprehension. She was in the thick of things. There was no one she could confide in. She knew no one who could accept or perceive a parallel paranormal world with its chathans and sorcery. Those who practiced the black arts would vie to eliminate her. If she spoke the truth, they would get her locked up for insanity. Chandy and whoever was with him would control the chathans. Tinku estimated that five chathans had gone over to the enemy camp. They were captive. It would take powerful magic to rescue them. Someone would need to pull out the nails from their heads. It would need powerful wizardry and potentially neurosurgical expertise.

Kusum decided to learn a bit of magic herself. She would learn from Chackochan's diary. She could spend some time in the afternoons in the loft. After the attempted dacoity, Kusum considered it ill-advised and potentially hazardous. Thomas would be on tenterhooks. He might let loose with his shotgun at imaginary intruders. Kusum decided to defer any forays to the old house at night. Thomas had hired a Gurkha watchman to patrol the fields at night. The wiry Gurkha with his bloodthirsty kukri was adequate insurance against invaders. It was expensive, but the midnight raid had thrown a scare. They also stopped letting out all the dogs together. Of the six Alsatians, they kept at least three chained at night. They would then be let out by the Gurkha. It would not be easy to drug all the dogs together anymore.

The next day was uneventful. There was a letter from Joseph. His company had promoted him and entrusted him with a new project. It was a prestigious and well-paid appointment. He would be tied down completely for the next year till the project was completed. Kusum wondered, why he ever married her. She realized that it was destiny. They were pawns in a cosmic duel. Kusum's entry into the Thoppil house was ordained. It was inevitable. After all, Chackochan had predicted all this a hundred years ago. After lunch when Thomas and Shalini went off to sleep, Kusum went up to the loft. She closed the loft door behind her. Tinku would help her open it when she wanted to go down. Tinku opened the box for her and she took out the little box with the black diary. Sitting on a small stool, she started browsing through the diary.

The book was written in Malayalam she could read it only slowly. As she turned the pages her stuttering incomprehension transformed into a eloquent understanding that was beyond the confines of any human language. The book assumed a life of its own and comprehension just flowed like a buzzing stream of crystal cold water from a perpetually brimming cornucopia of learning. The first few pages spoke of good and evil. Godly goodness had been gifted to humankind. The free will of humans implied that they were subject to temptation and desire. Desire was a double-edged sword. It fostered creativity and kindled change. Temptations drove the man to evil and sin. God's angels and Satan's hordes stalked the earth in mortal garb assessing and influencing their realms. The diary moved on to the history of the Kuttichathans. Created as God's helpers, they were banished from heaven for their mischief. Kusum nodded. This corresponded to what Tinku told her. The notes then went on to describe the enslavement of Chathans by the sorcerer's tribe. With the Chathans under their control, they wrought havoc. The erstwhile helpers of God were being used as Satan's agents. Sorcerers used Chathans to rob and harass people. Chackochan had worked out the magic spells to break the sorcerer's hold on the Kuttichanthans. The sorcerers got wind of this. There had been many attempts on Chackochan's life. The book then shifted from being narrative to instructive. Spells and chants and their espoused rationale were annotated. Spells were effective only if used by the right people and in an appropriate context. Evil could corrupt but not confront virtue. The best protection against evil was to be good.

Kusum was so engrossed in her book that she lost track of time. There was a small cough. Tinku was standing behind her. "We have made tea. Pappan will be coming back from the fields now". Kusum glanced at her watch. It was past five. She placed the diary back in its place. She got herself another book on physics from the box and went down. She sat that evening with Shalini and Thomas watching the stars emerge from the hideouts. She closed her eyes and felt a surge of strength. She understood why Thomas savored silence. There was power in silence. This stream of power was damped and fouled in the cacophony of meaningless prattle. After dinner, Kusum read her physics textbook. Tinku and the other kuttichathans fussed around her, getting her tea and snacks. They could sense her determination. She glowed with an inner fire. Tinku smiled. Kusum would be their saviour. Chackochan's premise and promise would fruition.

Chandy and his Empire:

On the terrace of his new bungalow, Chandy was holding a meeting. The lighting was subdued. Five little liveried chathan slaves served them exotic snacks and exquisite brews. Chandy was fuming. They had been bested by a young girl. Most of the chathans were free. The others on the terrace listened in silence. They were hard men. There was Davood. Davood was a smuggler and a drug runner. He ran a clandestine fishing operation. He synchronized and symphonized the smuggling of drugs from obscure ports on the Indian coast to stealthy merchant vessels in mid-ocean. The sealed boxes, packed with and labeled as seafood would reach their outlets in the west. At the other end, a QR code would assist the garnering of drug-containing parcels. Davood dominated the drug trade in the Indian Ocean region and complemented it with strategically incentivized and focused gun-running. Davood had supplied Tamil Tigers during the civil war in Lanka. He was now supplying arms to sustainable armed Maoist insurgencies in selected bastions across the country. The Maoists could pick up their weapons at the various fishing hamlets from Davood's boats.

Appu, the dacoit chief flitted around the forests of Andhra Pradesh and Karnataka. His gangs, ensconced in their protective cocoons of political patronage, ran extortion rackets, extending their tentacles into the metropolises of south India. They also controlled illegal logging and mining activities. Flanked by the two icons of violence was Aiyer, Chandy's partner in black magic. Their paths had crossed a decade ago at Madras. Both Chandy and Aiyer had been trying to restore the powers of a broken demon temple. They intuitively sensed their magical spells conflicting and prudently decided to merge forces. Together, they had released the temple's demon god from the chambers where he had been incarcerated for over a century. An obscure ramshackle hacked stone temple now bristled with primal vigor and strength. The power of the temple soon becomes legendary. Politicians and industrialists paid homage to the demon god with generous offerings of gold and cash. They begged the demon for political and monetary favors. The demon could proffer the power to sway people or eliminate real or perceived obstacles and rivals. The demon obliged. Chandy and Aiyer were trustees of the temple. They shared the proceeds with the Sadhu, who acted as the temple's caretaker.

Demon gods were not subject to control. But the demon was grateful to the sorcerers who had secured his release. A steady avalanche of finance would sustain their new strategies which pivoted from the pursuit of pecuniary interests to the pursuit of power. Chandy and Aiyer teamed up. Chandy continued his vocation as a professor in the university's philosophy department. Aiyer had relinquished his job in the bank and moved into full-time sorcery. Chandy leveraged his time, skills, status, and position to network and interact with various spiritual gurus from all over the world. Many mystics of massive repute and resources were frauds. Some of the esteemed and erudite seekers were scholars trying to understand the mysteries of the supernatural. They wrote papers and gave lectures. These academics were making a livelihood and accolades from their expositions and quests at the same time. There were some spiritual practitioners, as well as unsuspecting laity who had real or potential spiritual power. Chandy could sense these hidden forces within a man or woman. He had sensed the power in Kusum. He was intrigued by her innate unchartered power and wary of it. Subjugating her mind, body, and soul to his will was the essence and the raison d'etre to his passion to possess and tame her.

Chandy was wired into a network of sorcery around the world. This was an alternative universe that normal humans could sense but not comprehend. Sorcerers were powerful enough to influence the course of history. Over the eons, they had evolved from an abrasive force into an erosive one. They waited, corroding values, catalyzing conflicts, and igniting conflagrations. The battles between good and evil were zoomed into the collective human conscience. Human values and character would be subtly eroded till the color of the soul matched the hues of evil. The sorcerers would wait, confident that their time would come. A capable general knows his troops and is aware of the enemy's strengths. Chandy knew of Chackochan and the Kuttichathans. Chathans were a potent force if one had them in control. They could be a game changer. Unlike demons, chathans were basically good. Yet, with a magic nail into their skulls, they could be enslaved. A Chathan could be made to empty out a bank locker or puncture a dam and create a flood. They were restless creatures and had unlimited reserves and resources of energy. He had almost succeeded in bringing them to his camp. Kusum had stymied his quest. She had disposed of the silver key which had taken him a decade of magic to create. He would pay her back for that.

Chandy was impatient. The slow insidious erosion of man's virtue had continued over centuries. Chandy wanted control. Being mortal, the tide of time would ebb away from him. He had a plan. There was much to be done. The worldly ethos would need to be reset. For this, he needed raw power. He was desperate to have the chathans under his control. His friends had limited ambitions. For them, Chathans were agents of mischief. They could mess up the engine of a customs boat or create a landslide to drive back a posse of policemen. Chandy had a vision. His was a towering personality. Davood and Appu kept Chandy in front of their operations. He was their troubleshooter, philosopher, and guru. Chandy hid his true strength from them. His partners were after worldly possessions. For Chandy, worldly possessions were a path to eternity.

Heading an academic department in a prestigious institute proffered Chandy prestige and respectability. It was also a license to involve himself in research. Many of the leads Chandy followed were dead ends. Some, like the legend of the Kuttichathans or the leads that led to the unleashing of the power of the Demon temple, could pay rich dividends. Chandy realized that Chackochan's diary was key to controlling the Chathans. If he could lay his hands on it he could master the Chathans even without the magic key. Appu and Davood were keen to have another try at raiding Thomas' old house. Chandy cautioned them against this. The chathans would guard the diary fiercely. Unless their power could be taken away, at least temporarily, any raid would be foiled. Chandy evolved a fresh strategy. He realized that they would need to work their way through the household defenses. Kusum had been his first target. He realized that controlling Kusum would be difficult. He had some other nasty plans brewing.

The next few days passed without incident. Kusum ran the house well, with help from her little friends. In the afternoons, when Thomas and Shalini rested, she would spend time in the loft. She spends her time reading Chackochan's diary. She was developing an understanding of the world ethos from a perspective she never knew existed. Kusum was learning magic and memorizing the spells. Her understanding and awareness of the world around her was being transformed. She could listen to and commune with the voices of nature. Power came through understanding, realized Kusum. To control the elements, one had to converse with nature and gain her respect. The secret of this conversation with nature lies in respect and understanding. It all boiled down to being a good listener. Humans were too focused on themselves. Those who tried to listen ended up hearing echoes of their own voice.

There is an innate spirituality in Kerala. This is a spirituality that was palpable only to the sensitized. The hustle of materialism had numbed the sensitivities of most people to the rhythms of nature. There were a few fence sitters who were agnostic. Thomas was one of them. Kusum would enjoy sitting out in the evenings with Thomas. In the midst of the descending darkness, she could perceive the ebb and flow of nature's forces. Thomas could appreciate the change in Kusum. Her brashness had faded. She glowed with an inner mesmerizing maturity. His own son had been a disappointment. Joseph did not have in him the maturity which was an essential ingredient of greatness. Thomas only hoped that Joseph would appreciate Kusum's true worth. "Only those with eyes could see" thought Thomas. Thomas had the sensitivity to appreciate Kusum's growing strength. Thomas also sensed evil in Chandy and was wary of him. He was aware that Chandy was interested in their old house. He could also guess that Chandy's interest was related to black magic and sorcery. Shalini was totally oblivious to the sinister aspect of Chandy's personality. Moreover, she was absolutely enamored by his magnetism, personality, and sensually magical charm.

Chandy was making waves in the lecture circuit of Kerala. He featured often and prominently in the news. Chandy would be lecturing at the YMCA that weekend. Thomas saw the notification in the newspaper. He spoke about this in their evening's celestial séance. Thomas wanted to know more about Chandy's philosophy. Shalini too was all agog with enthusiasm and keen to attend this. Kusum was hesitant. She wondered how she would face him. The bruises of his assault were still fresh and the memories made her burn with indignation. Kusum made up her mind to attend the talk. Bodily bruises were transient. Mental resilience was paramount. An inner strength could absolve the physical degradation of an assault. Chandy would be speaking. The tone and content of his disposition would provide clues to the content of his character. The more you know of your enemies, the safer you are. Shalini of course was rhapsodic with excitement. She found Chandy ever so intuitive and intelligent.

The auditorium has a seating capacity of around 300. The hall was almost full by the time they reached it. The attendee list had been whetted by Chandy. He even finalized the seating arrangement. Chandy had a reputation for being a forceful speaker. There were unconfirmed rumors that he had spiritual power and influence over the devil. It was common knowledge that many icons in business craved his blessings before starting out on new ventures. There were also representatives from the Church. Chandy's initiatives in merging Hindu mysticism into the practice of Christianity had stirred a cauldron of controversy. There were many who believed that the future of Christianity lay in integration into local Cultures. Indian culture was accommodative and inclusive. A few religious fringes were the exception. As Chandy stood upon the podium, his piercing eyes scanned the crowd. They came to rest intrusively upon Kusum, making her squirm with embarrassment. There was a delay as the old computer in the hall struggled to handle his presentation. The technicians were called in. They would connect Chandy's laptop directly to the projection system. Chandy mounted the lectern. The lecture was on. "There are two issues I always had trouble with," said Chandy. "Women and Computers, I keep pressing the wrong buttons and having them hang up on me". The crowd roared with laughter. He seemed to look straight at Kusum. She was sure that he was mocking her.

The presentation started. Chandy spoke about the traditional Gods of the Dravidians and their demonization after the Aryan invasion. Chandy analyzed the inroads made by Christianity. English missionaries focused on education and empowerment of the deprived sections of society. A Kerala avatar of the Anglican church blossomed under British patronage. Christianity in Kerala merged with the existing temple culture, borrowing from Hindu traditions, values, and customs. Temples and Churches shared festivals and elephants. Islam, on the other hand, had been hostile to any attempts at integration. There was religious harmony and mutual respect. It was gracious and heartening that all religions were tolerated by the benevolent Hindus of the day. The values of Christianity and the traditions of Hinduism were synchronized and complementary. The talk went on and on. There would be plenty, for the local paper to talk about. Kusum was a bit disappointed. Chandy had not delved into the magic and mysticism of the South. She realized that this concoction of religious ferment was a front or a façade Chandy was creating. A façade of an enigmatic philosophy could veil and conceal murky undertones of black magic and sorcery.

After the talk, there was a tea party in Chandy's honor. The crowd milled around Chandy. There were autograph seekers and fans and a fair number of enamored women. Chandy's eyes were scanning the crowd. His eyes locked on Kusum. He was edging his way towards Kusum and Shalini but kept getting buttonholed by journalists and by the local intelligentsia. Shalini was dragging Kusum by the arm. "Let us go and meet him," she told Kusum. "The press is taking photographs. Our photograph too will come in tomorrow's newspapers: Chandy was watching them from the corner of his eye. The moment they came close, he turned to Shalini with a great show of affection. He praised her cooking and her hospitality. She was the epitome of a good Christian wife and mother. He seemed to be deliberately ignoring Kusum. He called for a photographer to click the three of them together, putting one arm each around both the ladies' shoulders. Kusum could feel the heat of arousal through his hand and squirmed. Chandy was intrusive and insistent as he deliberately and suggestively kneaded her shoulder. The power and passion of his personality were decadent and discombobulating. Kusum was grateful when Thomas came to their rescue. He had sensed Kusum's discomfiture. They had to excuse themselves despite Shalini's recalcitrance. Kuttappan had another assignment. They would need to drive back.

<u>The Sorcerer's New Strategy:</u>

That Sunday, after church, Chandy got himself invited for lunch again by Shalini. Kusum was determined that she would not let him out of her sight. Chandy however seemed to have no mischief planned. There were no requests to visit the old house. He kept the three of them enthralled with discourse. Kusum had locked the loft door and kept the key on her person. Even if Chandy managed to give her the slip, he would not be able to make it to the loft. Chandy was enquiring about Joseph. Shalini was bragging about her son. She glowed with pride as she reveled in the reflected glory of his recent promotion Shalini then started off about Kusum and her engineering college achievements. Shalini went on at length about Kusum's qualifications her academic aptitude and research interests. Kusum felt uncomfortable. Chandy was phishing and Shalini was giving away too much information. "Kusum is not working now, because we need her at home", said Shalini. By the time Chandy left, Kusum was uneasy. By now she was convinced, that he was hatching some plot to get her away from the house.

That afternoon, in the loft, she told Tinku her concerns. Tinku reassured her. No one, not even a sorcerer, could open Chackochans box without the key. Tinku always kept the key on his person, carrying it with him wherever he went. For added security, the Chathans would nail the box to the loft floor with interlocking magic nails. With the box nailed down, no one could shift the box even if they did manage to get into the loft. Kusum finished her magic lessons for the day. She returned the diary to the box, locked it, and handed the key to Tinku. The Chathans then got to work. One of them brought forward a box. Gingerly, Tinku opened it. Kusum peeped in. The box was full of gleaming writhing silver nails that hissed and snarled as the chathans picked them out one by one. Tinku hit one of the nails on its head with a silver hammer. The nail stiffened as it was driven through the side of the trunk and into the wooden floor of the loft with three smart blows. Other devil nails followed. Soon the trunk was neatly bolted to the loft floor. Kusum felt relieved.

Three days later she got a letter from Joseph. She opened and read this surprise missive with some trepidation. As she read on, her face brightened as a grateful luminescent smile lit up her face. An international university close to where Joseph worked, had advertised a job opening. The post of lecturer cum research associate seemed to be tailored for Kusum. Joseph's letter was brimming with uncharacteristic resources and enthusiasm. If they could find a caretaker to look after his parents, he would take Kusum to Dubai with him. Kusum blinked. The picture was too perfect. The conductor of this orchestra had not missed a nuance. Soon Kusum realized that this was Chandy's move. He had orchestrated events to stark perfection. Kusum would be with her husband and in a dream job. Her translocation to Dubai would move her out of the equation in Kerala. Thomas's will would wilt in front of Chandy's incandescent drive. Shalini would soon be eating out of his hand. With Shalini on his side, he would get the Chathans. Kusum had the premonition that Chandy would then come for her. He would come to possess her to assuage his ego.

Kusum analyzed the scenario. If she did not rise to the bait, Chandy would come up with some new diabolical plan. Kusum realized that it would be a loser's strategy to try and repel an enemy's attacks without evolving. A persistent aggressor would assess your defenses and wear you down. It would be brave but wise to pick up the gauntlet and fight afresh. There were many positives and myriad unpredictables if she took up the assignment. The job was exactly what she had wanted all along. Chandy read the situation well. He was offering her a lifeline of comfort and academic fulfillment. Would she take it and turn her back to her ordained destiny? Could she take up the job and still protect the Chathans? She relished the challenge. She was too embroiled in the mystery of the loft to walk away. If the family wanted her to go and be with Joseph, there was no way out for her. She could only hope that a suitable caretaker would not be found. Thomas and Shalini discussed the issue at lunch. They were happy about the offer and the prestige it offered. Kusum would be earning as much as her husband. The University was distinguished. She would have the opportunity to do research. Thomas and Shalini had another concern. There were some unsavory rumors about Joseph's social life. A scandal could be brewing. Kusum could get him back on track.

Thomas spread the word. They were on the lookout around for a 'live-in' help. It was not easy to get someone reliable. Days whizzed by. Kusum grew confident that they would not find anyone. After church that Sunday, Chandy was at their place for lunch again. At lunch, Shalini told him about the job offer Kusum had received. She boasted about Kusum being a loyal daughter-in-law. Kusum had refused to leave them alone in their old age infirmity. She would not leave unless someone really reliable who would look after Thomas and Shalini could be found. Chandy had a solution. He knew of a young widow. Her name was Reena. She had no place to stay and her in-laws were harassing her. She would fit the bill perfectly. Chandy would do the negotiations. He would bring Reena over the next day. Shalini could interview her.

Later that afternoon, Kusum held another council of war with Tinku. Chandy managed to ease her out and move one of his people in. With Kusum out of the house, the safety of the box would rest solely on Tinku's shoulders. Tinku reassured her. He was confident that the diary would remain safe. He would guard the key with his life. No sorcerer would try to open the box without the key. If someone broke open the box, the magic would be lost. The diary would disappear down a bolt hole in a black hole to the netherworld. Tinku looked confident. Kusum was concerned. Could Tinku hold out against Chandy's sorcery and machinations?

Things were moving too fast for Kusum's liking. Chandy had brought in a travel agent who was super-efficient. Kusum's ticket had already been booked. Her visa was fast-tracked. Shalini organized Kusum's wardrobe and travel bags. Reena the housekeeper had moved in. She had volunteered to sleep in the old house. Kusum was aghast. The old house had to be kept locked. Kusum spoke to Thomas. He agreed to keep the old house locked at night and to keep the key under his supervision. Reluctantly Reena agreed to sleep in a spare room of the new house. She was capable, polite, and seemed to have limitless reservoirs of energy. She kept the house and premises spic and span. She kept Pappan in his place and Mary on a short leash. Shalini was quite taken in by Reena. The dogs were somehow petrified of her. They would raise their hackles and growl when they saw Reena. Kusum soon sensed that Reena was not who she claimed to be. There was no doubt in her mind, that she was a Yekshi – a sorceress. Kusum did not visit the loft or take out the diary anymore. It was too dangerous. In the evenings, after she closed her room doors the Chathans fussed around her. The chathans had never moved out of South India. They would not be able to visit her in Dubai. Tinku was looking more and more preoccupied by the day. The responsibility of keeping the key safe was eating into him. If Chandy managed to get him and took the key, the battle would be lost.

Time whizzed by. The day of Kusum's departure came. Thomas and Shalini were at the airport to bid her goodbye. Reena was at home. The flight would take off in the early hours of the morning. Kusum sat at a corner seat in the departure lounge. There was no one close to her. She felt a sudden tug at her finger. It was Tinku. Holding a finger to his lips he pressed something into her hand. It was the key to the box. He was entrusting their safety with her. Without this key, no one could steal the magic of the Chathans. She kept the key in her purse. When she turned back, Tinku had disappeared. She boarded the airplane with a heavy heart. She had with her three of the latest issues of the Technology Updates' drawn from Tintu's loft library. She glanced through the pages. There were fascinating glimpses into the cutting edges of technology. Artificial intelligence was offering new paradigms of understanding in astrophysics. The resilient and transmissible data storage and retrieval capability of computers armed with machine learning would be key to unlocking codes and secrets of the universe and maybe of creation and the creator himself over time. After an hour she closed her eyes in meditation. Her mind was in turmoil and she could not focus on reading any more.

Joseph met her at the Dubai airport. There was little rapture or rhapsody in their reunion. They were from different worlds. Josephs lip sacking carnal drives and the genuine affection she felt for him were not complementary or in concord. Kusum sat in the cab with Joseph and looked out of the window. She was fascinated by the city sights. The city was futuristic. It was like a space station or a Mars settlement in the middle of the desert. They reached an apartment complex in the suburbs. Joseph stayed in a flat on the 13th floor. The apartment was not posh but definitely functional and reasonably comfortable. The construction, the lights, and even the interiors were tastefully done. They spend the day in the flat. Kusum told him about the home and the attempted burglary. She carefully kept out all the bits about the loft and its secrets and about Chandy's mischief. Joseph was curious about the necklace she was wearing. "It was my great grandfather's," said Kusum. "I never take it off". It is my lucky charm". "It seems to work", said Joseph. The post at the University was a prestigious one. An associate had noted their 'openings' notification and forwarded it to Joseph. Joseph had put in Kusum's CV on the last day. She was unbelievably lucky to have been selected. They slept after a bout of dutiful intimacy. Later, when the sun went down and temperatures cooled they explored the malls and shopping arcades of this desert paradise. The ability of the Arab world to preserve its sociocultural identity amidst a deluge of modernity was unique. While others had sacrificed religion and customs a tolerant yet rigid orthodoxy had prevailed here. Other traditions and socioreligious practices had receded into artefactual obscurity. Islamic culture, piety, orthodoxy, and garb persevered and even permeated liberal metropolises like Paris and New York. Joseph picked up a takeaway Mughlai meal from an Indian restaurant as they walked back to the car. On their way back, they drove past the campus of the university Kusum would be joining. Back at the apartment, Kusum got her documents and wardrobe in order. Joseph would drop her to the institute the next morning, on his way to work.

Kusum starts Work:

The university campus was cosmopolitan. A few Burkha clad women and young men in their traditional robes reminded one, that this was the Middle East. Most young men and women sported Western attire. The campus was aesthetically landscaped with lawns and fountains. Joseph had dropped her off at the administrative block. An attractive secretary wearing an elegant head scarf had asked her to wait for the dean. Kusum was given a brochure on the university. She leafed through it to familiarize herself with the institute's ethos. The university with its promise of scientific propriety and cultural prosperity was the pet project of the Emir of Dubai. The faculty of the university was mostly borrowed or stolen from the West. The University boasted state-of-the-art libraries and laboratories. Of late, they had started hiring younger faculty from the East and from India. There were a fair number of students from Asia. It made sense to have a resonant faculty, who could mentor and mold international students for relevant reintegration into their national ethos. The emir believed that emigration was a loser's choice. You should rebuild your nation and ignite its aspirations, not run away to welfare sanctuaries. Kusum checked the time. The Dean would be calling her in for her interview soon. After that, she would be free for the day. Joseph was at his office. She would give him a call when she was ready to return home.

A bell tinkled. She was ushered into the Dean's chamber. Richard, the dean, stood up and gave her a 'namaste' as she entered. A bit flustered and flummoxed, she smiled. They shook hands over his office table. Richard was from England. A former Professor from Oxford, he had moved to Dubai on the emir's personal request. Richard had been to India on many an occasion, both on vacation and for work. He had been charmed by the pristine beauty of Kerala. "We were impressed with your credentials", he told Kusum. "I have a weakness in your part of the world." He continued. "At the faculty selection committee, I rooted for you, so that you could tell me more about Kerala and its culture". Richard seemed to be a genuinely nice person and Kusum took an immediate liking to him. He explained to Kusum, as to what the nature of her duties would be. Kusum would mentor the engineering students, guide them in their practical work, and chaperone their research projects. She would be expected to bring out at least a couple of peer-reviewed scientific papers every year. Kusum would get an opportunity to present her work at international conferences. Kusum glowed in eager anticipation. This was the dream job she had fantasized about. In the aura of her rapture, flashed a sliver and a twinge of guilt. Kusum found herself wondering how the Chathens were faring. She was sure that they would find a way to contact her if they needed her. She had the key to the Chathans' box and controlled their destiny. Chandy would be furious to know that Tinku had given it to her. Kusum was confident that he would never risk damage to the trunk's contents by tinkering with the lock or by cracking open the lid. Control of the kuttichathans was key to his grandiose ambition and presumably for the execution of his sinister, diabolical plans.

The interview was over. Richard was expecting a visit from the education minister and would be busy with him in a bunch of meetings till evening. Kusum could use the library if she so desired. Her library was a revelation. Designed for functional excellence by an Egyptian artist it combined the rigid cataloging of Western bibliophiles with the languorous ardor of classical Egyptian erudition. Time whizzed past. Kusum called Joseph up at around lunchtime. Jet lag and the excitement of the past few days had drained her.

Joseph dropped her home and returned to work. She would have to knock up some lunch for herself. She opened the refrigerator, wondering what to cook. She felt someone tug at her jeans and squeaked in fright. There was Tinku. Your lunch is ready, he said. There, on the dining table, her warmed-up lunch was waiting. She laughed out loud and lifting up Tinku in her arms kissed him hard on the forehead. "I missed you so much," she cried. "How did you manage to come here?".

While she had lunch, Tinku told her all that had transpired. After Kusum left, Chandy had arranged a backwater boat cruise for Thomas and Shalini. It was a ploy to get them away from the house. When Thomas and Shalini were away, Chandy and Reena had opened the loft. Chandy had a magic stick with him to drive the chathans away. They had found the box nailed to the floor of the loft. Chandy inspected the lock on the box and cursed. He recognized it for what it was. If someone broke the lock – the contents of the box would be lost forever. He summoned the Chathans he had enslaved. He learned from them that the key custodian was Tinku. He had Tinku summoned. When he heard that the key was with Kusum he flew into a rage. He had beaten Tinku with his magic stick. Only the sound of Thomas' car made him stop. Thomas and Shalini had returned early. There was a spot of nasty weather brewing and the boatman had turned back in the interest of safety. Chandy fumed. He had been foiled again, by the girl. It was a stalemate. Thomas had seen Chandy's car parked by the porch. He looked suspiciously as Chandy emerged from behind the old house. Reena emerged from the terrace where she had been inspecting the laundry. Chandy made a polite conversation with Shalini and Thomas. He had seen the weather update of a storm brewing. He came, he said, to check out whether they had enjoyed the boat ride and were safe.

That night Tinku set out for Dubai. He smuggled himself into the luggage compartment of an international flight. It was icy in the hold and he caught a whopping cold. Tinku planned to stay on in Dubai, as long as Kusum was there. If he went back to Kerala Chandy would beat him black and blue every day. He was not strong enough to resist Chandy's sorcery. "Don't worry about Joseph finding me", said Tinku. I know how to make myself inconspicuous. Tinku had been busy cooking and cleaning. The house was spic and span. A delicious aroma of classical Kerala cuisine emanated from the kitchen.

Joseph was impressed with the dinner waiting for him. He had no idea, that Kusum was such a wonderful cook. There was a letter from home. The news from home was all apparently heady and heartening. Thomas and Shalini will be getting an internet connection soon. The cables had been laid. They should be able to communicate regularly within a week. The house was running smoothly under Reena's able hand. Fences had been repaired. The garden was weeded and spruced. Reena was very efficient. The dogs however did not like her and Thomas had to take over the job of leashing and unleashing them. Shalini was very pleased with her new help. The laundry was done on time and the ironing was exquisite. The food could not have been better. There was some more good news for her. Chandy bought a plot of land near their house and would start building a house there soon. Shalini was thrilled at the prospect of having such an illustrious neighbor. Chandy's academic outreach endeavors were gaining momentum. He had been invited to give a series of lectures on Indian Spirituality and would be touring the Middle East in a couple of months. Kusum shuddered when she heard of Chandy's Middle East tour plans. This was bad news for her and for Tinku. Kusum had been feeling relatively safe in Dubai. If Chandy was coming, he would be coming for the key. The lecture tour would be merely a ruse – Kusum was sure that.

The days passed quickly, Kusum was very happy at the institute. She soon grew popular with the students. The boys were in awe of her. The girls adored her. Kusum was petite and pretty without pretensions. She was principled with an enviable work ethic and a sharp intellect. She was competent enough to be honest about her capabilities. When she got stuck on a problem, she was honest enough to admit it. Students appreciated her candor. Richard took pains to ensure that Kusum integrated smoothly. He was always willing to help. He reached out with support, whenever Kusum floundered. With Tinku's help, the home ran smoothly. Joseph was away on tour, to construction sites much of the time. Kusum had the house to herself and spent her spare time at home, reading.

Thomas and Shalini telephoned. Their phone and internet connections had been installed. Kusum could ring them up a least a couple of times every week. Kusum's parents had translocated to Bangalore. Kamal, her brother, had completed his studies and graduated with an engineering degree in computer software. He had attended campus interviews and had been campus selection to an IT firm. Kamal was very close to his mother. She was justifiably proud of and ludicrously happy about his accomplishments. Kusum was aware of and vaguely resented the notion that their mother doted on him. Her mother would want to follow him as long as she could. By moving to Bangalore she could continue to mother him till he got married. She was busy searching for a girl for him. Kusum sighed at the thought. She hoped that she would get a decent sister-in-law. In that regard, she felt safe. Their mother would try to make sure that their future daughter-in-law was appropriate. Kusum had never been very close to Kamal. She had always been daddy's little girl and had doted on her dad. Her father was not too well now. His memory was failing him. Kusum hoped that he was not suffering from Alzheimer's. Her mom had always been the boss of the house. With dad's failing faculties, her mother's domination over family affairs was complete.

Kusum felt sympathy for her parents. They had returned to Kerala to set down roots close to their extended family. Dad and Mom were from a generation that considered caring for aging parents the sacred duty of their children. Times and values evolved. Grown children were on their own with their careers, concerns, and ambitions. Her brother would have no interest in nor show any inclination toward a return to Kerala. Her parents would be alone. There were relatives who stayed in the vicinity. The relatives were old and vulnerable too. Hired help was exploitative. They would extract as much money from you as they could. Sometimes live-in help could be potentially dangerous. Aging was frightening when you were alone. Your vulnerabilities were apparent to all. Your abilities were ignored by an impatient younger generation. It was not always this way. There was a time when elders were venerated. Society evolved. The era where old patriarchs were involved in decision-making was over. There was something to be said for a joint family system after all. Problems and controversies were settled and solved without rancor or litigation Conflicts and conspiracies were confined to the four walls of a house. Joint families were insurance against calumny and calamity. The old and the young would be wrapped in a protective cocoon of close relatives. The system was collapsing now. Young people were moving out, looking for better jobs and smarter spouses. A new order will be established in time. "When I grow old, I will probably need to move into an old folks' home," thought Kusum.

Joseph had to move out of the city for his project work. He was busy at work and otherwise engaged. He would come home once a month at best. Kusum was happy alone. She had her work and she had Tinku. The university kept her occupied. She wished she had more time on campus. There were a bunch of campus activities she could lead or take part in. In a year, they would give her a house on campus. Till then, the college car was available to drop her at home and to pick her up. It was not advisable for women to drive alone in Dubai. The university was cosmopolitan. On campus, she could lead a normal life. Outside, in the city, a single Indian lady moving about alone would raise eyebrows and much else.

Joseph's visits home were strained and uncomfortable for both of them. Joseph was constantly in a hurry to go away. Kusum was secretly disappointed in her relationship with Joseph. There was little communication and definitely no magic between them. Joseph was constantly unhappy and perpetually preoccupied. He was struggling in his job. He seemed out of his depth in his new appointment and was desperately trying to hold his own. At home, Tinku was Kusum's constant companion. Kusum just had to rub her pendant and he would come. They discussed Philosophy and he started instructing her in magic. With Tinku, Kusum understood the difference and progression of learning processes. Information is all around us. However, humans have the ability to be selective in their information assimilation. We sieve through the flow of information picking up nuggets of relevance and interest. Information becomes knowledge with application. Wisdom is knowledge tempered and flavored with personality, values, and character. Spirituality involved communion with the almighty and was a unique human attribute. Magic and sorcery were all about tapping into the streams of flowing energy all around us. Most people never sensed these streams. If you had the gift and tapped the positive streams you could do good. If you tangled with the negative forces, you would get irreversibly drawn into a cesspool of wickedness. The Chathans were denizens of the positive energy streams. They had access to all the information and knowledge archives. Chathans had information. They could perform any assigned task to perfection. They were gifted with the ability to acquire information and knowledge but were denied the elixir of wisdom. Wisdom invokes the exercise of free will. Wisdom was a divine endowment exclusively for man. Chathans had no free will or volition. They had been created as helpers. What they did, depended on their master's wisdom and disposition.

Encounter in Dubai:

The realization that Chandy would be coming to Dubai ignited a sense of urgency in Kusum's magic lessons. Learning invokes both inspiration and aptitude. Aptitude evolves from the availability and quality of learning templates in our genome. Not everyone can learn magic. Kusum had the gift. She was aware by now that her destiny would be crafted in the incandescence of her special powers. Every evening after dinner, Tinku would sit across the table from Kusum and instruct her. The magic she was learning was being etched into her genetic code. Kusum started maintaining a diary and taking down notes. Tinku made a concealed magic chamber under the dining room table. He would hide the diary in this chamber after Kusum finished her lesson for the day. The chamber with its invaluable content would be appreciable and accessible only to him and to

Kusum. Tinku got Kusum a small jeweled box. This was for Kusum to keep the key to the Chathan's trunk which had been nailed to the floor of the loft. Kusum had no idea where Tinku slept. When she was alone at home he was always with her. He cooked and shared meals with her. When Joseph or anyone else came home, Tinku was just a shadow. Only Kusum could sense his presence.

Six months went by. Kusum relished the accolades and appreciation she received at the university. One of Kusum's research papers was accepted for presentation at the Pan-European conference. The scientific content was not Kusum's original work. Richard gave her the leads and access to his data. Kusum had compiled his work at the lab over the previous five years. Tabulating and analyzing the data had been hard work. Richard was pleased with Kusum's diligence and with her intuitive interpretation of the results. It is the aspiration of every professional to achieve his or her potential. Kusum was happy without complacency. Joseph was not too enthusiastic about his wife's new-found eminence. He exerted his resentment by ignoring her accomplishments. Joseph threw a few tantrums. He, like most Malayali male bullies, was meek and ineffectual at his workplace and a tiger at home. Kusum was amused and irritated. When she refused to be intimidated, Joseph sulked. He got himself a new girlfriend and stayed away from home often. At home, he turned docile and pretended to be preoccupied.

The pan-European conference where Kusum's paper was to be presented was scheduled in Paris. Kusum attended the conference with Richard. He was always a thorough gentleman, introducing her to other scientists as 'my brilliant young researcher from India". Richard had been through a messy divorce a decade ago. He had been wary of women ever since. But Kusum's straightforward candor put him at ease. He was comfortable with her but took care not to intrude into her personal space. Kusum's paper was appreciated. After the presentation, there was a deluge of interest and a barrage of questions. The interest evinced spilled over to the reception in the evening. Later there was a flurry of emails and queries. "You have now moved into the major leagues", Richard told her. With this presentation, your views and opinions have become scientifically visible. Now, if you say something, the scientific community will listen.

Kusum and Richard got back to the University on Monday morning. Richard had a scheduled meeting with the Procter. He got dropped off first. When Kusum went home to drop her bags and change, she found Tinku in a tizzy. "He is here, he is here", he kept saying. "Who", asked Kusum, her antennae whirring in alarm. All the elation of a great conference dissipated and her heart sank as she assessed the peril. She knew who Tinku was talking about. "Sorcerer Chandy", said Tinku. "He came in the morning and rang the doorbell. He knew that I was inside. I told him that you were out of town. I told him the truth. He wanted me to open the door. I did not have the key to the front door. He was furious. He will be back in the evening". Tinku was looking sorely agitated and very concerned. "I will not be able to protect you from him. His magic is too powerful. Stay at the University tonight". Kusum was not going to be cowed down by Chandy. "You have taught me a lot of magic", she told Tinku. "Don't worry", I can take care of myself". Kusum had a relaxed breakfast. Tinku rolled up his eyes in resignation tinged with awe. He had crafted a secret chamber on the floor under the dining table. He placed the loft key with Kusum's Diary with her notes on magic in it. He then rolled out a carpet over the floor and stuck down with magic spittle. The secret chamber with her diary and the key was well hidden. No one could get at it, except a Chathan.

Kusum telephoned Thomas and her parents, to tell them that she was back. Thomas told her what she already knew. Chandy was in Dubai. There was something else. Chandy had offered to buy their house for a very handsome price. Kusum was furious. "No way," she said. Don't sell the house at any cost. She knew what he was after. If he managed to get the key to the box from her, he could use their house as a headquarters of his sorcery. "Chandy is very well connected in Dubai". Thomas continued. He has offered to put in a good word to Joseph's boss. "I think he might have influenced your appointment also". Kusum was startled. It was all very possible. She realized that Chandy could have used his influence in Dubai. "Why would he do that? Did he just want her out of Kerala? Was he also planning to enact a personal whim or vendetta upon her away from the militant uncertainties of Kerala polity?" She would buttonhole Richard on this today. She had an uneasy feeling that she would require his help soon.

That afternoon, during lunch break, at the faculty dining hall, Kusum found herself alone with Richard. "Have you heard of a professor of Philosophy from India, one Mr Chandy", Kusum asked. She tried to sound casual. Richard gave her a long hard look. "I have heard of him", he said. He is supposed to be very close to the Emir and is very influential in Dubai. This morning, I heard that he is in town". Richard was looking at her. Kusum had to say something. "He is not a very nice man", she told Richard. "But he knows my people in Kerala. If he comes to meet me I want to know how to shoo him off". Richard knew of Chandy's reputation as a womanizer. But he had seen and assessed Kusum's character and capabilities. He was confident of her ability to take care of herself. Kusum's obvious consternation, however, made him wary. "Why don't you stay on campus for a couple of days" suggested Richard. Kusum would not agree. She could take care of herself. "Well, if you need me, just speed dial me on my mobile". Kusum smiled as he took her telephone and registered his number for emergency calls. Kusum was confident she would not need it.

She reached home late that evening. There had been a presentation by her students and a discussion on the synopses from the Europe conference. Dinner had been laid out in the auditorium foyer. Kusum was exhausted. She excused herself with permission from Richard and declined the invitation to dinner on campus. Party food gave her a headache. She wanted to talk to Tinku and reassure him. Tinku would knock up some dinner for her. Besides, she wanted to talk to Joseph and to the folks at home. She was dropped home by the University's staff limousine. Kusum had a feeling that she was being followed. She was tempted to tell the driver to turn around and drive back to campus. It would have been prudent to stay on campus. If she went back at this late hour, many people would be inconvenienced. Kusum grits her teeth in quiet determination. The driver would wait till entered her apartment. There was a van parked down the road with tinted glasses rolled up. She could not see if there was anyone inside.

Kusum went to her door. It was locked from the outside. She unlocked the door and opened it. She then turned around and waved to the driver that all was well. The car moved off. Quickly she locked the door from the inside. She then put on the light. The room was as she had left it. But where was Tinku? Kusum walked into the dining room. The table was not set. Had Tinku gotten scared of Chandy and run off without telling her? Kusum was a bit irritated with him. She opened the refrigerator brought out a precooked meal and put it into the microwave. She would telephone Joseph first. She picked the telephone off the hook. There was no dial tone. The phone was dead. There was a public telephone down the road, but she did not have the courage to go out on the road again. The parked van was worrying. Besides, it was unsafe for a woman to venture out of her house alone, after dark. Her mobile telephone had only local connectivity. On an impulse, she picked up the telephone to ring up Richard. She would reassure him that she was safe.

Kusum stiffened, feeling a movement behind her. A powerful hand clamped across her mouth and another encircled her waist. The telephone slipped from her hands and fell. Even without looking, she knew, it was Chandy. He was a powerful man. Smothered in his excruciating warmth her breath came in short gasps. Her body burned in blistering arousal and her struggles were futile. It took him just a minute to subdue her. He threw her down on a chair. She sat there, numbed. He would have entered through the front door with an access key. Once inside the house, his accomplices would have locked the front door from the outside again. What had happened to Tinku. She hoped that he would have had the sense to hide. She regretted not having called Richard earlier. In another few seconds, she would have speed-dialed him. She looked around for her mobile. It had fallen to the ground, but she could not locate it. Chandy had drawn a chair, up close in front of her, prizing her knees apart with his. His warm breath caressed her face as he looked deep through her eyes into the recesses of her mind. "We would make a great team", told her. "I want you and I want the key to the box". Seeing the look of fear in her eyes, he continued. "Let us start with the key. Why don't you tell me, where you have hidden it".

Kusum was desperately trying to remember the magic spells Tinku taught her. She could feel Chandy's probing finger in her brain. He was trying to subdue her and read her thoughts. Desperately she fought back. With her silent chants she wove a magical web. She repulsed his mental probes. She created a fire-wall that Chandy could not penetrate. She could feel the pendant she wore glow, amplifying her strength. Chandy sensed it too. He sprang forward. He held her by the neck with one hand. With the other, he tore open her blouse and ripped off her necklace. He put the necklace in his pocket and then released her. Kusum sank back sobbing into the cushions.

Chandy was using all his mental powers now. Kusum's defenses were crumbling. She felt the claws of his evil tear through the webs of her mind, probing deeper. Kusum was faltering in her magical chants now. Each time she faltered she could feel his grip over her mind tightening. She would succumb to him in a minute. Suddenly there was a crash as the front door was kicked in. Chandy rose to his feet with a start. Kusum fell back on the sofa, ravaged by his intrusions. Richard, accompanied by three burly security men burst into the room.

Richard took in the scene at a glance. He looked at Chandy. "We meet again", said Richard. The security men had moved in and grasped Chandy's arms. Chandy did not seem scared at all. He was sure of himself, confident that his influence at the palace would bail him out of any situation. Richard seemed to sense this. "These security men are from the university. If I tell them, they will shoot you and ask questions later". Chandy looked worried. Search him, ordered Richard. The men found Kusum's broken chain and handed it to Richard. He looked at it and without a word passed it to Kusum. "Let him go", Kusum pleaded. If the news of his arrest in her apartment reached Kerala, it would create a distressing scandal. Richard understood. "We are shifting you to the university campus. If you want, we will tell your husband that there was an attempted burglary". Kusum nodded. "It is a good thing you telephoned me" continued Richard. Kusum frowned. She was sure, she had not managed to dial his number. She remembered her missing mobile. Tinku must have grabbed it and speed-dialed Richard. He had saved her yet again.

Richards Story:

The security men marched Chandy out of the apartment. He gave Kusum a malevolent stare as he passed. Richard helped Kusum to get her stuff together. One more car had come from the university, with some of Kusum's lady colleagues. They took over the packing, while Richard talked to Kusum in the living room. He told her the circumstances when he first met Chandy. It was at an archeological site in Egypt.

Richard had been invited by the Egyptian government to study some newly excavated scrolls. He was staying at a makeshift but luxurious campsite close to the site of the dig. Richard was an early riser. Every morning, he would don his sneakers. He would jog out of the township and down the desert road. Later after breakfast, he would be taken to the archeological site in a luxury sedan. Deep in the recesses of a burial chamber were a series of rock inscriptions. Below these, secreted in a rocky recess were multiple scrolls. The scrolls and the rock carvings were linked. The scrolls seemed to have some mathematical formulae. Egyptian professors who studied the document could not decipher the meaning or the purpose of the calculations. Richard had pondered over the documents for three days. The mathematics had been exquisite. But it seemed to lead nowhere.

On the fourth day, Richard jogged a new trail. It was an ancient caravan route. Campsite lights receded behind him. In his hands, he had a photocopy of the scrolls ensconced in a silver quiver. He planned to sit in the sand at the halfway mark and study the script some more. The mathematical formulae in the scrolls resonated through his mind as he ran to its rhythm. A gust of cold desert air whiffed a puff of sand in his path. Other sand spirals sprang up in his wake. Ahead was a glistening veil of sunshine shimmering with morning dew. As Richard ran to the rhythm of the mathematical formulae on the scroll the ebb of time on the sands around him slowed to a crawl. He was shrouded in a time warp. He found himself astride a majestic white horse in an oasis. In his hand, he held a scroll. He was surrounded by masked men on black horses with drawn swords. As the masked men closed in Richard swirled the open scroll in a scintillating shield. Numbers like darts flew out of the scroll enveloping the masked riders in a plume of white flame. As the numbers flew out of the scroll his enchanted universe faded. Richard found himself back on the camel track. He was exhausted, drained emotionally, and dehydrated. Abandoning all thoughts of a halfway break, he jogged back.

Richard turned back dazed. He walked and jogged back to his hotel. Had he hallucinated? Was there something magical in the numbers on the scrolls? It struck him that the documents were formulae for enchantment. Richard was a religious man. He was wise enough to realize that he was tangling with forces he would not parlay with. That morning, at his makeshift office at the archeological site, he summarized his findings in a report. He telegraphed his report to the minister in charge. He also requested that he be relieved of further work in the field. The minister acquiesced. It would take a day for his return to be arranged. Richard spent the rest of the day summarizing his data and collecting photoprints of the scrolls and inscriptions. The data was black magic through numbers. The news of this find must have leaked out. Richard and his team had been camping near the site. That night, he had sensed some movement in the desert. He got up quietly and crept along the shadows to the sentry post. He found the sentry, with his throat slit. The sentry's guns were gone. There was another sentry post higher up on the Pyramid. There had been a carnage here. Four sentries were lying there in pools of blood. Richard had quietly wired for help from his pocket transmitter. If he raised an alarm, they would all possibly get massacred.

The army unit, positioned twenty kilometers away would come to their rescue. Richard had crept back to the campsite and alerted his team. He told them to scatter into the desert and lie concealed till help came in. He then entered the tombs, where the scrolls lay. He could hear crashes as the raiders broke down the barriers one by one, as they made their way into the inner chamber. Richard took the scroll and escaped into the secret passage just before the last door came down in a cascade of dust. Concealed in the passage he had watched the scene below. There were four masked bandits wielding automatic weapons. Behind them was a man dressed in the flowing robes of an Arab Sheikh.

Richard recognized the man in robes as Chandy. Chandy had taken a quick look at the empty box in the chamber. He had looked around and then barked an order to his men. The men had started searching the chamber. Richard withdrew slowly into the passage, looking for an avenue to escape. Suddenly there was a commotion in the room. A shot was fired. Richard peeped back in. The soldiers had arrived. They rounded up the bandits. There was a major in charge. Richard had met the major earlier at the consulate. Holding the scroll in his hand, Richard emerged from the passage calling the Major by his name.

The major recognized him. He held up his hand signaling that Richard was a friend. Richard held out the parchment. "They were after this". He showed the Major the scroll. The bandits were cuffed and taken away. The Major questioned Chandy. Chandy claimed to be a researcher who had been taken hostage by the bandits. Richard knew this was untrue. Chandy had been in charge. There was a burst of gunfire in the distance. Richard immediately deduced what had happened. The bandits would have been eliminated. There would be no witnesses left. The Major was helpless. He took Chandy into custody.

It took Richard and his team two weeks to secure the site. Later, he contacted the major before leaving the site. The Major had a dire tale to tell. A team of gunmen had accosted his soldiers who were escorting the bandits in custody. The prisoners had been freed and asked to run. The bandits had run into the desert only to be downed by a burst of submachine gun fire. There were no other witnesses. Some powerful Sheiks had intervened to get Chandy released.

Murder in the Desert:

Kusum's friends finished her packing. She was glad that she had not got Chandy arrested. He was powerful in these parts and would not only have gone free but also got her into trouble. She would be safe on campus. She remembered the box under the dining room table. Leaving her friends outside, she went back in to collect it. Tinku was sitting on the table holding the box in his hands. "I almost thought you forgot this," he told her. Go on, I will join you at your new apartment on campus. Kusum wrapped the box in her sweater and returned to the car. When they reached the campus, her apartment was ready. She hid the box with the sweater wrapped around it in a corner of the clothes cupboard.

One of the students had been down to the cafeteria. He was back soon, laden with pizzas and coke. They had a good meal together. Richard and her friends left. Kusum locked the door from inside. She heard some scurrying sounds. Tinku emerged from under the bed. He seemed happy. Together they chose a good hiding place for their box, in the living room safe. There was a small chamber inside, which was not immediately obvious upon opening the safe door. Tinku is framed in an illusion to render the chamber imperceptible to intruders. They then hid the safe key in a corner of the clothes cupboard. These measures were probably unnecessary on campus, thought Kusum. Chandy would not come into the campus, she was sure of that.

After all the excitement, Kusum slept well. Tinku woke her up in the morning with a cup of tea and biscuits. She rang up Joseph and told him that she had shifted to the campus. There had been an attempt by someone to break in, while she was in Europe. Joseph did not seem too concerned. She also rang up Thomas and her parents. She told them that she had shifted to campus, but did not mention any attack.

That day, during lunch break, Richard asked her. "What was it that Chandy wanted from you?". Kusum blushed. She would have to tell him at least a part of the truth. "I will tell you over the weekend", she told Richard. "It is a long story".

As usual, Joseph would be busy during the weekend. One of her friends had suggested that he was probably seeing a girlfriend. There was this girl from the Philippines, who worked as a nurse in the Dubai hospitals. Kusum realized that she did not care. She was only worried about the folks back home. If she and Joseph were to formally split, they would be devastated. She was sure that Joseph understood this equally well. She was being pampered by Tinku. He had repaired the pendant's necklace for her. Their magic classes were on again. She learned a lot, from her last encounter with Chandy. There was a lot of work she would need to do to make herself stronger.

Chandy returned to Kerala. He had to rework his strategy. There were other issues he had to tie up. The land allotment for his ashram was under scrutiny. There were some activists who wanted transparency. The conundrum could be resolved with a little finance. Activists had to live. Their children deserved good and often expensive education. These were minor irritants and money could solve most problems. His vision for the world and the path to its transformation had evolved a locus of clarity. Control of the chathans was critical. Chandy wanted the old house with its loft and the magic trunk. He was pestering Thomas and Shalini to sell their old house to him. Thomas, on Kusum's prompting, had refused. The loft and the box should not belong to Chandy, even if he did not have the key to its secrets.

That weekend, Kusum and Richard had driven off to a seaside resort. Richard had booked separate rooms for them. They met in the morning at the beach shanty for breakfast. Kusum told him the whole story. Initially, she was worried, Richard should not think that she was crazy. But he was attentive and seemed to understand what she was speaking about. He had ordered lunch and the story had continued over lunch. Finally, it was over. Kusum felt a great weight off her chest. She had finally found someone she could confide in. They drove back in the evening to the campus. Dinner was at the cafeteria with a group of friends. Kusum returned alone to her apartment. She had work to do. In addition to the magic lessons, she had to prepare her lectures for Monday.

Tinku got dinner early for her. Kusum was totally dependent on him now. He would join her for dinner when they were alone — sitting awkwardly with his plate balanced on his lap on the floor. "You told Richard about us folks, didn't you?'. Kusum nodded. "He is a good man", said Tinku. Kusum was relieved. Tinku's appraisal was reassuring.

The week was hectic. Joseph had called once to say that he would not be able to come down that weekend too. Thomas called her up every evening. Kusum felt closer to him than to her own parents now. Chandy had visited them again. There was no mention of his encounter with Kusum. He averred his inability to call on her and had not mentioned anything about his visit to Kusum's house. His brimming agenda included visits to the ruling elite and prestigious conferences. He had again tried to convince Thomas and Shalini to sell the old house and move to town. Chandy chose for the couple, a dream penthouse in an affluent apartment complex. The penthouse with a ten-year maintenance contract and a generous bank balance to offset maintenance costs was offered. Thomas had demurred politely and then refused outright as Chandy piled on the pressure through assorted well-wishers and through Shalini.

Kusum knew that Thomas would do nothing without her consent. He seemed to have little faith in his son's judgment. On the other hand, Shalini was all praise for her son. The son however rarely rang her up and Shalini was chagrined and had to have to depend on Kusum for information about him. Kusum herself knew little about her husband's whereabouts. Kusum would try and be diplomatic and cover up for Joseph. She sometimes wondered how this parody would end. The unraveling was sooner than she expected.

Some of Kusum's friends had seen Joseph with his girlfriend at a beach resort. Kusum realized that this might have been going on for some time. Joseph had been having an affair with this girl for some time even before his marriage to Kusum. She would not bother to find out. She realized that life was too complex to unravel in a hurry. She would just have to play it out and see how things evolved. Professionally Kusum was happy. The conference in Europe had given her a tremendous impetus. She enjoyed her work and was focusing on two major projects. With Tinku managing the house for her, she could stay at the lab till late into the night. At home, a warm dinner would be ready and she would spend time with Tinku and his magic lesson before sleeping. In the morning, Tinku would wake her up with a hot cup of coffee. He slept under the dining table. With Kusum in the next room and the keys in the safe. Tinku felt reassured. He was in touch with the Chathans in Kerala. They had told him about Chandy's attempts to buy the old house. Thomas had refused, but they were still worried. Chandy was always looming in the background and his agent, the new maid was hovering about the loft. But with the key safe with Kusum they felt secure.

It was Wednesday and Kusum was ready to leave for work, when the telephone rang. It was from Joseph's company. He had not reported to work for the past two days. "Did Kusum have any idea, where he was". Kusum was stunned. She could not ring up Thomas. There was nothing Thomas or Shalini could do. Had there been an accident? She tried Joseph's mobile number. The bell rang but there was no response. Kusum walked down to her office. She was to give the second-year students a lecture on nuclear physics. With her mind in turmoil, she managed to finish her talk and then went to Richard's office. She told him, what had transpired. Richard immediately took charge. He summoned a faculty member to reschedule his and Kusum's lectures for the rest of the week. He spoke to the institute director. He could take Kusum and drive across the county to Joseph's office. The drive would take four hours even on those wide-open desert highways. The institute had provided a Ford van. The air conditioning was effective and it had a refrigerator with enough water and food to last a couple of days. The institute had offered to provide a driver, but Richard had declined. Their plans were still fluid and he loved driving himself.

Kusum packed a small bag with her clothes. Richard too had lagged along an overnight bag. He had brought his pistol along. They would be off the main highway for a good part of the drive. There were bandits in the desert, there were also rogue tribes who would rob, rape, and murder without compunction. Fortunately, the drive was uneventful. Richard had kept a steady speed and the wagon zoomed through the desert roads at a scorching pace. Finally, ahead of them, they could see the township where Joseph's construction firm had its office.

They had driven straight to the company gates. Richard had given the security guard his credentials. The gate was opened and a guard had driven with them, to the manager's office. The manager had heard of Richard and was obviously in awe of him. He had no clue of Joseph's whereabouts but called in an employee who oversaw Joseph's department. This colleague turned out to be an Indian. His name was Patil. Introductions were made. Patil seemed to be in some discomfort. Richard sensed that there were possibly things he did not want the senior man to hear.

He offered to take Richard and Kusum to the apartment where Joseph lived. On the way to the apartment, he told them all that he knew. Joseph had left on Sunday morning for the resort which was a hundred miles away. The resort was a popular haven for young couples and it was likely that he had left with a girlfriend. He was looking at Kusum as he spoke. "I know about it", said Kusum. Joseph and his friend had not returned as they had planned on Monday morning. The hospital where the girl worked as a nurse had also been making inquiries.

They reached the apartment. The building secretary had a spare key to the apartment. Kusum, Patil, and Richard had opened the front door. The flat was empty. Joseph's briefcase, which he had carried back from office was lying on the living room table. The refrigerator was well stocked. In the bedroom, there were two cupboards. A woman's clothes and a nurse's uniform hung in the cupboard. Joseph had been living with his girlfriend. Kusum was biting her lip, to keep her emotions in check. They locked the flat and dropped Patil back to his office. Richard procured a map of the area and studied the roads to the resort. They telephoned the resort. There was no one by the name of Joseph who had registered over the weekend. He must have checked in under an alias, guessed Kusum. They would drive down to the resort the next day. They spend the night in Joseph's apartment. Richard slept on the couch in the living room. Kusum despite her misgivings managed a good night's rest on Joseph's bed.

They started out across the desert again. The roads were narrower. There could be sand dunes and the occasional oasis in the distance. Only a couple of cars crossed them on the road. At the resort, they had gone to the manager. Again, Richard's name seemed to carry a lot of weight. No, there was no one by the name of Joseph, who had checked in. The clerk, who had manned the desk on Sunday was summoned. Kusum had a photograph of Joseph in her purse and they had obtained a photograph of the nurse from her hospital. The clerk identified them immediately. The couple were frequent customers and had registered under the names of Ajith and Farah Singh. They had checked out on Monday morning as usual. They had driven down in Joseph's car, a small Toyota compact.

The clerk remembered that someone else, an Arab, had also enquired about this couple. He seemed suddenly on his guard and was not willing to tell them anything more about his Arab. The manager asked him something curtly in the local dialect. The man nodded and was allowed to go. After he left the manager turned to them. I am afraid, that the news is not good. The Arab was a notorious gangster. If he had made inquiries, it was likely that there was a contract raised against Joseph. Joseph would probably be dead and the woman sold off to some Sheikh's harem. Kusum was trembling now. Joseph was, after all, her husband. Worse, she did not know what and how to tell Thomas and Shalini.

Kusum is kidnapped:

Kusum was given a room, where she could rest. Richard, meanwhile made some enquiries. Fortunately, the police chief was a friend of his. Through the police contacts, they had quizzed the Arab. It was as they suspected. Joseph had been killed and his body had been disposed of. The orders for this hit had been given by a Sheikh Omar whom Richard heard of. Omar was Chandy's friend and the two had been hand in glove in their botched-up raid on the Egyptian scrolls. If Sheik Omar had wanted Joseph dead, it would be on Chandy's orders. Why would Chandy get rid of Joseph? In a second, he realized that Kusum and Joseph's parents were in danger. With the family out of the way, it would be easy for Chandy to gain possession of their house, with its loft and the Chathans. Quickly he returned to the resort and went to Kusum's room. He knocked a the door. Kusum opened the door, bleary-eyed. She had been crying, but she was safe. Richard told her all that had happened. They tried to phone up Thomas but no one was answering. In desperation, Kusum rang up her brother Kamal. Kamal was in Kerala on a business trip. He would drive down to Thomas' place and confirm that all was well. He would convey the news that Joseph had met with an accident and had been probably abducted by bandits.

Richard and Kusum waited at the resort till the police came. The police chief told his men that Richard was an academic of National importance and a sincere friend. All assistance should be offered to them. The detectives weighed the evidence. They were not optimistic about tracing Joseph's body. The desert was large and a body could be easily disposed of. A woman who disappeared into the harems could never be traced. The only clues could be on finding the car. Even that was unlikely. The bandits would first drive across the border and sell it. Number plates and registrations were easy to change. There was nothing to be achieved by staying at the resort. They decided to head back to Joseph's apartment and spend the night there. The next day, they would head back to the university. The police captain did not want them to drive alone. Bandits could stop and rob a single car. A police car was sent to escort them back to town. They reached Joseph's apartment before midnight. There had been no call from Kamal. They would get a few hours of sleep before dawn and then head back to the university. Richard had instructed his agent to book Kusum on an afternoon flight to Kochi. She would need to meet Thomas and Shalini and spend some time with them.

Richard slept on the couch. Anxiety and angst had stymied restful sleep the past few days. There was tragic clarity. He was intensely sorry for Kusum. She meant the world to him. Tomorrow, when they were both rested, they would strategize and formulate an action plan. He was in the deep dreamless sleep of exhaustion when something nudged his senses awake. He was sleep-deprived and disoriented. It took him a couple of minutes to realize where he was. It was still dark. He wondered what had woken him up. Then he heard the sound again. It was the creaking of a window sill. He was sure all the windows had been closed. He stiffened. Someone was getting into the apartment through the window.

Jumping out of the bed he padded across to Kusum's bedroom door. It was open. He could make out the silhouette of a man moving towards Kusum's bed. As lunged to protect her, he heard the swish of a club behind him. There was a dull thud. The last thing he heard before crumbling to the ground was Kusum's muffled cry as her attacker gagged her.

Richard was coming to. He had a throbbing headache. At first, he had no idea as to where he was. He was lying on the floor of a room. He raised his hand gingerly to the back of her head and felt the caked blood. The apartment looked familiar. Daylight was streaking in through an open window in the room ahead. There was an empty bed ahead of him. Suddenly he remembered. Where was Kusum? He groggily got up on his feet and searched for his mobile telephone. He found it in the pocket of his jacket, which was draped over the sofa arm. Quickly he dialed the police chief.

Tinku was in a tizzy. He had stayed on at Kusum's apartment on her instructions. He could sense that something was going wrong. Kusum was in trouble. He needed to do something – but he would require help. He meditated and contacted chathans in the loft. They had their own tale of woe. The news from Kerala was disconcerting. There was trouble across multiple theatres. Chandy's gang had used the five chathans they controlled to rob a bank. The other chathans were powerless against Chandy's magic. The threat at home was dire. The chathans were sure that he was planning to harm Thomas. Thomas had refused to sell the house to him. Chandy was seething. Tinku told them that Kusum was in trouble. He would need their help to rescue her. Five chathans would come to Dubai. They could move around invisibly and would make their way to Dubai in any available transport. That left ten chathans to guard the loft.

The Chathans decided to row across the sea. A fleet of fishermen stared in astonishment as a wave sliced through their nets at high speed. They could not see the Chathans on their little catamaran. They surmised that some sort of big fish had cut through their midst. Some of them disagreed. It had been too fast to have been a fish. Was it some sort of freak wave or some missile launched from some submarine? Anyway, fishing for the night was over. Their fishing nets were tattered. They sailed back into the fishing port. The Chathans homed in on Tinku's mind waves. It was still dark when they reached Kusum's university apartment, where Tinku sat waiting. Tinku rose as they drifted in through the closed window. He quickly briefed them on what had happened. Joseph, Kusum's wayward husband was missing and probably had been murdered. Kusum had left with Richard to investigate. She was in trouble. They would have to find her soon and rescue her before anything horrible happened to her.

Kusum meanwhile was lying trussed up on the floor of a large van of some sort. The men who kidnapped her had muzzled her with a chloroform-soaked rag till she stopped her struggles and lost consciousness. Now, she was slowly coming to, vaguely conscious and distraught, still dazed from the effects of the drug. The van she was in was large and she was lying on some sort of a rag. Someone had rolled up blankets on either side of her. Whoever had kidnapped her, had not wanted her damaged. Deliberately she kept her eyes closed. She did not want her captors to know that she was awake. They seemed to be driving cross country, probably across the desert. She wondered what had happened to Richard. She had a vague memory of seeing him falling down at her bedroom door before she passed out. The van was coming to a halt. She could hear voices outside. The back of the van swings open. In the dim light of early morning, she could see some sort of a desert camp. There were armed men walking around, rifles slung over their shoulders. She was lifted out of the van. A burly man, who seemed to be the tribal chief. With strong hands, had slung her over his shoulder and carried her to a tent. He put her down on a soft feather bed shrouded with silk curtains. A shimmering fine satin pink kaftan was laid out for her. On a golden footstool was a crystal jug with sparkling wine and two crystal glasses. The chief eyed her with rapturous adoration. He turned around and barked at his men. "Tell the sheik his trophy is here", he instructed. He turned back to Kusum. "I will be back when the sheik leaves". Kusum was alone in the tent. Her captors left. She opened her eyes and looked around. She sped a jug of water on a silver tray near the door. She sat and drank some of it. It was cool and refreshing. She felt strangely calm.

A fresh drama was being unfurled in the middle east. Tinku and the other Chathans set out towards where they sensed Kusum would be. They left the city roads and were soon in the wide desert. A swirl of desert sand was the only visible sign of their move as they raced across the sand dunes. Some camels broke into a trot as they saw the furious chathans. Camel drivers looked quizzically at this new type of sandstorm and muttered to each other. "The ways of the desert are mysterious".

Kusum could hear the sound of voices growing nearer. There was the snorting of horses. She peeped out of the tent. A white stallion has stopped outside the tent. A regal-looking tall Arab dismounted as his assistants steadied his horse. The leader of the armed group, the one who had carried her to the tent, was greeting him. They embraced each other. The armed man pointed toward the tent. The Arab turned towards Kusum's tent. He was a handsome man, with an aquiline nose. A scar ran down his cheek to his mouth, giving him a cruel look.

The Arab took a step towards the tent., but the leader of the band stopped him. His man had brought a laden table forward. There was wine and food on it. There was no way the Arab could refuse the hospitality without offending the man. He sat with the leader under the palms. A flask of water had been brought for him to wash his hands. The men ate and talked. Suddenly Kusum felt a tug at her hand. She glanced down in alarm and almost laughed loudly in relief. It was Tinku. Behind him was a whole bunch of smiling Chathans. Kusum pointed to the men sitting at the table. The handsome Arab was glancing impatiently at Kusum's tent. He was eager to possess the latest acquisition of his harem. His hosts were finally getting the message. They stood up in deference as he got up and belched. They got him a bowl and a white towel to wash and dry his hands.

They moved aside as he walked towards the tent. The Chathan's had got busy. An avalanche of sand rose in a raging sandstorm and headed into the oasis. There was now a wall of swirling stinging sand, like a million stinging hornets between the men and the Kusum's tent. Men ran for cover. Horses bolted. The Arab sheik impatiently shielded his face and stood behind a palm tree. Kusum and the Chathans escaped from the back of the tent. No one could see them. Tinku led Kusum to a clearing behind the oasis. The van in which she had been brought captive was parked there.

A Chathan wearing a chauffeur's uniform was sitting in the driving seat. Smiling, he pointed to the ignition key and moved out of the driver's seat. Kusum got in and started the engine. The chathans hopped in behind, giggling in excitement. Behind, the wall of sand was settling. Kusum gunned the engine and turned the car, in the direction Tinku pointed. Behind her, she heard the sound of shots being fired from the Arab's pistol. The rifles were choked with sand and could not be used. The poor visibility also protected them. The car with its sand tires surged through the desert. An hour later, they had reached a highway.

Richard had been given first aid in a nearby hospital. He was then driven hack to the university under escort. He was lucky to be alive. Kusum's abductors must have had orders not to kill him. It was easy to get away with killing and kidnapping Asians. Africans did not count at all. But with Europeans and with American citizens' it was a different matter. The press raised one hell of a stink and the countries were bound to seek some retribution. Richard was very upset about Kusum. The girl had trusted him as his eyes brimmed with sorrow. There was a click as the front door opened. He spun around in alarm. There she was, radiant in the glow of adventure and glowing with expectation. He took her in his arms in a caressing crushing rapturous embrace and smothered her sun-baked lips in a long delicious kiss. They stood, lost in aroused rapture for a long, long time. The wait was over, the agony had been worth it.

<u>A symphony of synchronized violence:</u>

Kamal had never been very close to his sister. But what she told him had troubled him deeply. He was a hundred kilometers away from Thomas' house and his work at Kochi was unfinished. He decided to finish off his business visit. He would then drive down to Thomas' house and convey the news that Joseph was missing, in person. He had been out of Kerala for a longish time and the roads would be unfamiliar. With a bit of roadside assistance, he was sure he could find the way. Kamal tried to ring Thomas on his land phone. The mobile phone revolution was yet to reach the innards of Kerala. Thomas' telephone did not seem to be working. He gave his driver the necessary instructions. Their return drive to Bangalore would be delayed by a day.

Thomas and Shalini were getting ready to retire for the night. Their new maid had taken the night off to visit her relatives. Thomas was feeling uneasy. The dogs were restless. When he let them out, they had refused to run around the courtyard but sulked around near the kennels, their tails between their legs. He had half a mind to call some cousins over, but they would think he was paranoid. Chandy's insistence on buying their house was disconcerting. The money he offered was good and the flat he was getting for them in town was an excellent one, with all amenities. Kusum had been adamant, that the house should not be sold. She had been so insistent, that Thomas realized that there was something she had not told him. Thomas' faith in Kusum's judgment was complete. The last time Chandy had brought up the topic, Thomas had given a flat no. He had discussed it with Joseph. He averred that Joseph had told him not to sell the old house at any price. This was a lie. It had been weeks since he spoke to Joseph. If he realized that his lie resulted in Joseph's untimely and violent demise he would have been discombobulated.

The house lights had been switched off. Shalini had gone to sleep. Thomas picked up the telephone to dial his cousins. There was no dial tone. The phone was dead. It might have been dead for a while. He remembered that there had been no incoming calls throughout the day. Through the open window, he could see lights moving across the courtyard. The dogs were barking and growling in the yard. There was a knock on the door. Shalini had woken up now. There was another knock and then Chandy's voice, "Open, it is me, Chandy".

Kamal dozed in the car as his driver drove on to Kottayam. The business meeting had gone off well. It was dark now and he knew Thomas and Shalini were early sleepers. He felt remorse over delaying his visit. He could have driven straight down to their house to tell them about Joseph's misfortune. The scheduled meeting had been an important one. He was aware that there was little Thomas or Shalini could have done with the information. He had received no further calls from Kusum. On the way, he tried unsuccessfully to ring up Thomas. It felt a bit cruel to wake up an elderly couple and tell them that their son was in trouble. He wished Kusum would call up. Maybe she would get some good news before he reached Thomas' house. Kusum's telephone was again unreachable. He wondered what he could tell them. He decided he could just tell them that Joseph was missing. He could be with the old couple till Kusum called again. Kamal rang up their mother in Bangalore. He told her of Kusum's call. Kamal's dad was unwell. His Alzheimer's had been worsening. There was no point trying to tell him anything. His mother would try to ring up Kusum from her telephone. She agreed with Kamal's plan. It would be better if he conveyed bad news in person. Kamal checked his watch. It would take him another hour to reach the house.

Thomas opened the door, with Shalini standing behind him. Chandy was in black trousers and a dark-colored shirt. Behind him was a group of dacoits armed with lathis and sickles. Shalini screamed and fainted as the men rushed in and seized them. They gagged her and threw her on the bed. Someone put scotch tape across Thomas' mouth and dumped him on a chair. Chandy pulled up a chair and sat opposite him. He opened his briefcase and took out a sheaf of documents. "Sign here, Thomas", he said in a terrible voice. You don't want to see your wife suffer. Thomas looked around. One of the men had opened a can of petrol and was splashing it over Shalini. Another had taken a matchbox in his hand and was holding it ready. Thomas glanced at the document. It was a deal transferring ownership of his house and property to Chandy. His heart sank. He was wise enough to realize that Chandy could not let them live after tonight.

A hail of stones came in through the open window. A stone struck the man holding the matchbox. He sank to his knees, holding his bleeding head. The chathans were trying to protect the old couple. Chandy picked up his stick and charged out of the room. The chathans scattered as he flayed them with his magic whip. The men were helping their injured comrade to his feet. Thomas picked up the document from the table and tore it into shreds. Too late, the man realized what he was doing. One of the men knocked him senseless with a lathi. But the damage was done. Chandy had come back into the room. He flew into a rage when he saw the torn papers. He had planned to get Thomas' signature before he killed them and burned down the new house. The murders would be made to look like a dacoity and he would claim that the deed had been signed a week earlier. He had ordered the elimination of Joseph. He had plans for Kusum and wanted her alive and captive. One of the dacoits came running in, "There are cars coming up the road. One of them is a police car".

Kamal's car reached Kottayam town. He had a vague idea, of where to turn off the road to head for Thomas's house. However, in the dark, none of the landmarks looked familiar. They were outside the town in the countryside now. After half an hour of aimless driving, he had to accept that he was completely lost. He wished he had stopped in town to ask for directions. There were few houses around and no one on the roads. They stopped the car by the roadside. Ahead they could see the lights of an approaching vehicle. Kamal got out of his car and waved to the driver of the oncoming vehicle. As the lights got closer Kamal realized that it was a police jeep.

The jeep screeched to a halt. Apologetically Kamal went across to ask the police officer for directions. He smiled in pleased surprise. The police officer was an old friend of his. They had attended school together. He remembered the officer's name, Ravindran. They used to call him Ravi. Ravi had recognized Kamal. He got out of the jeep. Kamal told him about Kusum's telephone call and how he had lost his way to Thomas' house. Ravi called one of the policemen from the jeep who was from the locality. This policeman knew Thomas' house. It was on the other side of the town. Ravi offered to escort Kamal's car. He got into the car with Kamal. Kamal's driver would follow the police jeep. Meanwhile, the two old friends exchanged notes. There had been a spate of dacoities in this area. Ravi was out on patrol to give people a sense of security.

The jeep slowed down. It was a mud truck ahead with no street lights. They drove across the paddy fields towards coconut grooves. Thomas' house would be behind a small hillock. Dark clouds deterred starlight this moonless night. There were no other houses in the vicinity. Kamal realized that he would not have found the place without Ravi's help. There was a yell from the jeep ahead. There was a fire erupting in Thomas' bungalow. Brilliant orange flames hissed and spluttered in raging anger. The two vehicles sped toward the burning building and stopped a safe distance away. The policemen and Kamal sprinted towards the burning house. In the light of the flames, they could see the old Kerala house that Kamal remembered. The old house was safe. The new building was on fire and smoke was pouring out of the windows.

One of the policemen spotted a water tank and some buckets. They started throwing in water through the windows to deluge and douse the flames. Kamal and Ravirushed to the front door. It was latched from the outside. Ravi kicked the door open. Inside, the bed was on fire and there was a strong smell of petrol. A motionless form was lying on the floor enveloped in smoke, Kamal rushed in. He lifted the unconscious man in his arms and carried him outside. It was Thomas. There was blood on his head and his skull looked distorted. Someone had hit him on the head with a heavy object. But he was breathing. Policemen got the fire in control. Ravi and Kamal rushed Thomas to the hospital. Thomas had suffered a severe brain injury. Shalini's body had been found. It was charred beyond recognition. Chandy had set them ablaze before escaping with the dacoits across the fields.

Kamal had rushed Kusum's father-in-law to the hospital in time. His surgery went off well. The surgeon was optimistic that Thomas would survive. Thomas recovered well. In a day's time, he was off the ventilator. In three days, he was being mobilized out of bed by the physiotherapist. However, he would have some loss of memory and it would take him a while to be able to speak.

<u>Restoration and Love:</u>

The flight from Dubai was landing at Kochi. Kamal waited in the visitor's lobby. Kusum had emerged through the emigration and customs gates. She walked across to the railing and stood with her brother. They waited in silence for a while, till Kamal's driver maneuvered his car close. Kusum had carried only a small box, which fitted into the car's boot easily. During the drive back, they talked about all that had happened. Richard had offered to come to Kerala with Kusum, but Kusum had dissuaded him. After things settled down, she would fly back to university. She promised to call him up every evening. Richard was worried about what tricks Chandy would try next. After Shalini's murder, there was a police sentry on duty near the house. Chandy would probably stay away. Besides, there were the Chathans. Kusum told Richard about the chathans. They would be returning to Kerala with her and would protect her. The Chathans never appeared before him. He had heard of the Chathans earlier and events over the past few days left him in no doubt that powerful forces were at play.

Kamal's car had reached the hospital. Brother and sister walked into the intensive care unit where Thomas was being treated. He had just come back from physiotherapy and was tired and drowsy. Kusum stood by his bed and called him softly. His eyes seemed to flicker open and there was a hint of recognition in them. Thomas eyes closed again. The nursing staff assured them, that he was stable. Kusum could visit him again later in the evening. Kamal took Kusum to an uncle's house where they had lunch. Everyone in Kerala seemed to have heard of Joseph's misfortune. They treated her with extreme compassion.

Shalini's body was kept in the morgue and the funeral would be the next day. The body was charred beyond recognition and the casket had to be kept closed. Kusum realized that she had been very fond of her. Thomas and she had understood each other well. Shalini too had been very kind and considerate, even if her judgment of people and events was occasionally flawed. Kusum stayed at her uncle's house. Kamal had to return to Bangalore to tie up some loose ends. They had driven to Thomas' house. The old building was locked and exactly as Kusum remembered it. The new maid had not returned and the police were looking for her. The dogs had gone into ecstasy on seeing Kusum. She had petted them and given them food. The new house had been damaged by the fire. Kamal had arranged for a caretaker to stay in it, while repairs were in progress. The police were also around and would send some of their men to sleep there for a couple of weeks. Kusum meanwhile stayed on at her uncle's house.

The funeral went off without a hitch. Thomas was recovering slowly. Kusum spent a lot of time with him. It was obvious that he recognized her. However his speech and comprehension were both impaired. Kusum could gauge that he had been through a lot. There seemed to be something he wanted to communicate. Without speech and with his right side weak, it was all bolted in. Sometimes he would cry silently, tears trickling down his cheeks, as though overcome with some deep inner sorrow. But when Kusum was around, he seemed to have hope. He would hold her hand while she sat beside his bed, eyes closed in silent prayer. Every morning Kusum would drive down to their house to supervise the work there and feed the dogs. She could sense that the chathans were in the loft. She would visit them after she could move back into the house. She spoke to Richard in the evenings. She told him that she would have to stay back to get things in order. Richard promised to keep her post open for her. He gave her some projects she could do at home. Her uncle's place had an internet connection and she could do some work online.

Months passed before Thomas' house was ready for occupation. Thomas was soon well enough to be discharged home. They had arranged for an elderly man who would move in with Thomas as a caregiver. Thomas was now able to move around his room with a walker. He could not speak clearly yet. He could, however, communicate his needs through words and gestures. The old man, Kesavan, would sleep in Thomas' room and care for him. Kesavan had grown up in the neighborhood. Thomas and he had fished and climbed trees together as children. Thomas seemed to instinctively trust him. He was most comfortable with Kusum or Kersavan around. Although Kesavan was Thomas' age his body was lean and hard with years of hard work in the fields. Kusum found him respectful, resourceful, and reliable. With Kesavan to support them, she was now ready to move back to Thomas' house. The house had been done up well. There was now an internet connection. With this and her mobile telephone, she could be in touch. The road to their house had been repaired and a new housing colony had sprung up close by, with a small shopping arcade and a community hall. The area was developing and their house was not as isolated as it had once been.

Kusum communicated regularly with Richard. Through Richard's connections, she had been invited to many institutions around South India to give lectures as visiting faculty. Chandy had shifted to an Ashram, he sat up in the hilly region of Idukki. The ashram was built like a fort with state-of-the-art security features. A large number of foreigners frequented to ashram. The Ashram had the pretentious title of 'International Center for Vedic Research'.

Kusum was sure that Chandy was behind the murderous attack on Thomas and Shalini. The police however had no incriminatory evidence and Thomas was still neurologically too impaired to give any credible insights. Kusum had got herself a new car. It was a Fiat hatchback. She soon got used to the roads, drivers, and traffic of Kerala. The roads were riddled with potholes and the traffic was disorganized. Many of the drivers were callous, loud, and uncouth. The police force was short on manpower and often stymied by politics and corruption. Yet there was some core goodness in the land and people were not vicious. Kusum felt safe driving around to various universities and colleges on her own.

They had shifted back to Thomas' house. Mary, the maid would come in the morning and finish off the housework by noon. Kesavan was always around in a supervisory role. Kusum had converted the room beneath the loft into a study. She had her internet connection here and an extension of the telephone. Her books were stacked neatly against the walls. Her room was always spotlessly clean. The Chathans were happy now, with their mistress close by. She spent some time every day in the loft, with Tinku and the Chathans. She was studying Chackchans diary again and she could sense that her magic powers were getting stronger. She would lead the chathans in meditation. Tinku was still wary of Chandy. "There is trouble brewing", he would confide in Kusum. Chandy and his henchmen were working on some major project. The five chathans he had abducted had not been heard of for some time. The dacoits had not made any major attacks for a while. It was all too quiet to be true.

Kusum decided to spend a couple of months in Dubai. Her university post was still unfilled although she had been away now, for a good six months. Richard had gotten her apartment done up. Kusum was looking after Thomas well. Thomas could speak a few words now. Kusum would sit next to him and talk about her work. He would listen intently. On a couple of occasions, she had tried to talk about Joseph and Shalini. Thomas' breathing got labored, he sweat profusely and his eyes had brimmed over with tears. Kusum had to quickly change the topic. She gave Kesavan instructions on how to contact her by telephone. She could now communicate with the Chathans using her magic powers. They could keep in touch.

Richard had driven down to the airport to receive her. She had missed him terribly. As they sat in the car, they held hands and talked. Richard told her about all the project work they had undertaken. Their department had received affiliation and accreditation from Harvard. It was a rare honor. She rested her head against his shoulders as they drove to the university. An impromptu reception had been organized for her in the executive restaurant of the college café. Her friends were aware of the stormy travails Kusum had survived. They exulted in the emergence of Richard and Kusum as a couple. After the party, Richard and Kusum returned to her apartment. The house had been redecorated. Kusums study was spectacularly organized with scientific books, an extension of the institute's internet, conference consoles, and screens. Kusum walked mesmerized into her bed chamber. The room had been hued her favorite pastel. In her cupboard was an assortment of office and Leisurewear. She opened the next, smaller cupboard. Richards clothes were stacked neatly. Kusum blushed and then flushed as she turned around. Richard flicked off the bedroom lights as they came together in amorous abandon. Later seated on her deck overlooking the campus lights, they talked late into the night.

The next two months passed quickly. Her students were ecstatic over her return. She would spend the whole day with them, guiding them in their work and inspiring them in every way possible. She spent her evenings with Richard. Their friends would drop in occasionally. They hardly ever left the university campus. Richard too had kept the news of her visit as quiet as possible. They did not know, what enemies they had outside. She would speak to Kesavan every day. Thomas was well. Tinku too assured her that all was well. He was still wary of Chandy. But whatever he was up to, he seemed to be in no hurry to attack them. A week before she was due to return, Richard proposed marriage to her. Kusum had declined. She loved Richard deeply and cherished the moments she spent with him. But there were things she had to do in Kerala. If she married Richard, her work with the Chathans would remain unfinished. Richard understood. He would wait.

<u>Kusum is readied for Battle:</u>

Kusum meditated and steeled herself on the flight from Dubai. The aircraft landed in Kochi in the early hours of the morning. She hired a cab to take her home from the airport. The sun was just peeping over the horizon. Kerala was already wide awake. There were children in school uniforms hurrying for tuition with looks of intense determination on their faces. New houses had bloomed all over and yet the greenery around was a real deep glowing green. Woman, their wet hair open, clad in traditional attire made their way back from the temple. A few retired elderly men in dhotis and donning sports shoes were returning from their morning walks. Dogs and cows jostled with humans for space on makeshift sidewalks, often spilling onto the road, causing her driver to slow down with a screech of brakes. They reached home by ten. Kesavan had prepared breakfast for her. Thomas too was sitting out on the porch. Thomas stood up clutching his walker, on seeing her. She ran across and hugged him. She was all he had in the world. Kusum felt her eyes brim over with tears. After BFast she went out and said hello to the dogs. They barked and bawled a rollicking welcome. It was nice to be back.

The house was as she had left it. There had been no further turbulence, no violence, and no shocks. Kusum wondered if the peace she perceived was real or was she, as Tinku insisted, in the eye of a storm. Kusum settled in. She worked late into the night on her computer that night. There was some unfinished work that she needed to complete. Thomas and Kesavan slept off early. The night was strangely quiet except for the occasional bark of one of her dogs as he chased a bandicoot down its hole. She had spent some time with Tinku and the Chathans in the loft, after dinner. They were happy, but there was shimmering subterrain excitement she could not fathom. Kusum wondered why they looked so happy. "Was it because of her return?" Kusum had a feeling that it was something beyond that. They were hiding something from her. She was back in her study correcting students' projects. She could hear excited whispers upstairs as the chathens chattered in excitement. Were they celebrating something without including her? Kusum felt a wee bit peeved.

Kusum finished her work. She yawned. She smiled as she remembered Richard. In their apartment, whenever she yawned Richard would seal her mouth with a wet kiss. The kisses and their follow-through had added to many an ecstatic night. Kusum had warned

Richard that incentivizing her latitude would make her lazy. The clock chimed. It was midnight. It was time for her to sleep. She felt a whiff of cold night air. The door of her study was opening slowly without a creak. She sat motionless, strangely unafraid. If there were any danger, the dogs would have barked and the chathans would have rushed to protect her. An elderly man, who looked strangely familiar, was walking in through the door. In his hand, he had a staff. Kusum was glued to her chair. The old man seemed to ignore her completely as he walked across the room and climbed the ladder to the loft. The loft door swung open before him. He was in the loft now. The trap door shut softly behind him. Kusum got from her chair. She had guessed who her nocturnal visitor was. It was Chackochan. She had felt her necklace heave as he walked past. No wonder the Chathans were smiling. Their savoir was back.

Kusum returned to her room and settled in. She felt strangely at peace. The return of Chackochan to the world of living was reassuring. She could focus on her science work now. She missed Richard and wondered what the future held for them. Tinku had got her the latest issue of the Journal of Nuclear Physics. He leafed through it in bed. There was an article from her university authored by Richard and her name had been included as a co-author. She smiled in satisfaction and drifted into sleep.

It became a routine every night. She would sit in her study working on her publications till midnight. Every night after the stroke of midnight her study room door would open and Chackochan would waft in noiselessly. After Chackochan climbed into the loft she would put out the lights and return to her room. Her mornings were busy. She would drive to wherever her lectures were scheduled. In the evenings, she would sit with Thomas and Kesavan during dinner and watch television. There has been a spate of terror attacks recently, in different parts of the world. Travel and tourism had slowed down. She received a call from Richard. He was safe. Most of the attacks had targeted big cities in the West. The Interpol was looking for a pattern, which could lead them to the terror mastermind.

After dinner, she would return to her books. A week had gone after Chackochan's first visit. Kusum sat in the study preparing her presentation for the Institute of Science. She had a busy day and was nodding her head sleepily over her laptop. She decided that she would, out of respect for the old man stay up till Chackochan's arrival. By midnight she was almost falling asleep on her keyboard. The door opened and Chackochan came in. As he walked toward the ladder to the loft, Kusum got up. She was ready to douse the light and go to bed. Something made her pause. She sensed that something significant was about to happen. At the first rung of the ladder, Chackochan stopped and turned around. He looked at her directly for the first time. Kusum stood, transfixed, staring into the deep grey kind eyes of the old man.

Chackochan smiled as he spoke to her for the first time. "Come, my daughter", he said. "Tonight, you join us in the loft for a while". Kusum was not sleepy anymore. She followed Chackochan up the ladder and into the loft. The loft was lit with little lanterns that the Chanthans had kept around a long table. Kusum wondered, where the table had come from. It had not been there before and anyway, it was too large to have been carried up through the loft door. The loft itself seemed to have expanded and the two of them seemed to be in some sort of a conference hall. A Chathan pulled out a chair at the head of the table for Chackochan. He sat down and motioned to Kusum to sit by his side.

There was a door at the far corner of the hall. Kusum and Chackochan waited patiently. Soon, the door swung open and men started coming in. Some of the faces looked strangely familiar. They all looked serious and scholarly. They seemed to represent all the great civilizations of the world. There were Chinese monks and Africans in their flowery robes. There was a Shinto priest from Japan and a Red Indian chief. There were Europeans. One man, very British in his demeanor, looked strangely like Richard. He walked over to her side. "You are right", he told her. "I am Richard's grandfather". Kusum remembered Richard speaking about his grandfather David. David was a

professor at Oxford before he opted for the holy orders. He was a great biblical scholar and a well-known philosopher. David died before Richard was born, but his photograph on the mantelpiece had always been an inspiration for Richard as he grew up.

There were about twenty of them around the table now. Tinku and the chathans got busy, pouring them some exotic fruit juice. It was an extract from a berry found in the Himalayas. Kusum found it delicious. They snacked on some delicious fruit salad. Each person was served a different cuisine by the chathans. "We are all set in our own dietary preferences", explained chackochan. "We come to the meet from our own homes, our own cultures. Our thoughts however share a common thread of humanity". Human intellect can neither be replaced nor rendered irrelevant. There is only one way for civilization to go and that was forward. Artificial intelligence can access and analyze available knowledge paradigms and evolve incremental advancements. The human brain is capable of conceptualization and creation of new paradigms. Human intelligence and AI were complementary. Humans would make great leaps of faith. AI would consolidate the gains and when necessary, mitigate the damage.

Many discussions were on. There was lively debate on Global warming and Geoengineering. Richard's uncle David summed up the conclusions. Creating a solar curtain with reflective suspended microparticles was effective in dampening global warming. Replacing the reflective particles with energy-absorbing microspheres was an option that could be evaluated. These energy-storing microspheres could be harvested in every diurnal solar cycle and replaced with a fresh cloud of beads. Meanwhile, the energy from the energized harvested beads could be streamed to the power industry and transport. The de-energized spherules would be hoisted back to the stratosphere for the next cycle. Researchers, working in diverse fields, whose work could contribute to the holistic project were identified. The job of nudging them together was given to Tinku and the chathans. They would harmonize serendipity to edge the researchers to coordinate their work streams. A daily harvest of solar energy, while reducing Global warming was an eminently desirable outcome.

Another concept was harvesting energy from molecular bonds. Nuclear fission could be replaced by molecular dissociation. Regionally focused desalination of seawater could be a source of endless energy. Molecular dissociation was less draconian and disruptive than nuclear fission or fusion and would have little military application. The desalinated water would be routed for human and agricultural use. There was another erudite discourse on the role of retroviruses in evoking phenotypic and intellectual changes in species. The doctrine of retroviral reverse transcription in tailoring genomes was nature's way of forging the evolution of species for adaptation in a changing world. The Darwinian concept of natural selection was a consequence and not the result of evolutionary mutations. Kusum listened in fascination to Nobel Laurette's and Philosophers debating and deciphering the enigmas and the conundrums of civilization. Time stood in deferred reverence to the content and context of the deliberations.

Kusum was now aware of a tic-toc sound as time started churning again. Chackochan held up his hand for attention. There was silence and stillness as the delegates paused their pondering to participate in the epochal keynote address by Chackochan. "Through the centuries", he started, in heavily accented but flawless English, "the balance between good and evil had been dynamic. The healing touch of good was the balm that soothed sufferings produced by man's cruelty. Indeed, the purpose of human earthly existence is to purify oneself in this cauldron, to emerge in a form acceptable for a heavenly presence. Every century there have been challenges to this delicate balance when the forces of evil have plotted to decimate goodness. These situations call upon specially chosen people, apostles you might call them, to rally the forces of good into battle".

He looked around. "We are all past it", he was speaking to others in the group. "We fought our battles. The world is, what it is today, because of our courage and sacrifice. We fought and we fought well and fair. We lost battles, but in the end, our wars were won. Today we are relegated to the sidelines. We have gallery seats in our heavenly abode to oversee and mentor bearers of our celestial mandate. We are on the verge of another battle and our General for the war is this young girl". Chackochan put his arm affectionately around Kusum. "My daughter", he continued. "I have no doubt in her capabilities. This war will be led by her. The gathering clapped. They streamed to Kusum to bless and congratulate her. The gathering dispersed. The lights dimmed.

When the light came back on, the loft was, as it had been before. She and Chackochan were seated on stools in the loft while Tinku perched on the box. The other chathans stood in line, as if on parade. On Chackochans prompt, Kusum acknowledged the Chathan's salute. Chackochan stood up and helped Kusum to her feet. "I will show you what I am talking about". "Close your eyes". He instructed Kusum. "Let me take you on a virtual tour of Chandy's new campus. Kusum closed her eyes, holding onto Chackochan's hand. The rest of the room faded from her consciousness. The misty night air streamed past as they zoomed into the clouds and headed for the hills. In a while, they slowed. They came down through the fluffy moist clouds with their silky caress. There were lights below. Ahead of her, she saw great brass gates. There was a marble archway. Over it, embossed in glistening gold letters was the logo, 'The International Center of Vedic Research'.

Kusum had heard about Chandy's center. This was the first time she was actually seeing it in all its magnificence. The walls were massive and topped with barbed wire. There were uniformed sentries at the gate. Chandy and Kusum wafted through the layers of security at the gate. The guards perceived just two puffs of mist drifting past. Chackochan was leading Kusum through the tour. There was a road leading through a densely wooded area. Ahead of them was some sort of a training ground. Here, a group of men were undergoing intensive commando indoctrination and training. "They train mercenaries at night". Chackochan told Kusum. In the daytime, they allow visitors here. The grounds are then used for yoga and meditation.

There was an old stone building straight ahead. On the first floor, the lights were on. Chanchan and Kusum reached the gallery and peeped in. Chandy was at the head of the table. He was bent over a map, giving instructions to a group in commando fatigues. "They plan their strikes all over the world here", Chackochan explained. There was a large map of the world on the wall. There were black crosses marked over various cities on the map. With abject horror, Kusum realized that these were the cities where terror strikes had occurred. There were a whole lot of other cities with red crosses. "These cities are targets for the strikes they are planning", Chackochan explained. The targets seemed to be random and across geopolitical and religious divides. "Terror has no religion", continued Chackochan. The individual foot soldier thinks that he is dying for a cause. Those who control the pawns orchestrate a sinister strategic menace.

Suddenly Chandy froze. He had sensed their presence. Quickly, Chackochan whisked Kusum away. The wind whistled as they zoomed out of the center and into the shrouding caress of the clouds. In a trice, they were back in the loft. "He will not follow us here", Chackochan reassured her. But he knows we are watching him. Fortunately, he does not know that you are the warrior chosen by us. Kusum felt a shudder of fright. If he did, she would be his target again. Chackochan smiled, we are with you and I will prepare you for the battle. They were back in the loft now. The conference table had disappeared as had the other visitors. Tinku was there. He had put two chairs astride the old box. They opened the box and withdrew Chackochans diary. We do not have too much time. But I will tutor you and make you strong.

Kusum's lessons in magic had started. Chackochans erudition was as scintillating as it was systematic. Information was the foundation on which edifices of knowledge could be built. The Garden of Knowledge was sprinkled with the wisdom of the sages. Learning was sequential and incremental. Power evolved from the wise application of knowledge. Information was available and the essence of synthesized worldly knowledge was accessible through the magic box. Chackochan provided the inspiration that was the essence of Kusum's education. The chathans kept busy tinkling with snacks, tuning music, and adjusting the virtual air-conditioning. It was almost five in the morning when Kusum came down from the loft with Chackochan. She went into the new house. Kesavan would be up soon. He would get breakfast ready. Meanwhile, she would sleep for four hours. There was a lecture she had to take in the local college at ten.

Kusum was making do with very little sleep. She would work on her science project and lecture till midnight. Every night, at the stroke of midnight, she and Chackochan would go up to the loft. There, with his diary open, and an avalanche of contemporary reference works drawn from the celestial library indexed in the magic box, he would tutor her on the majesty and mysteries of the mind. Magic was in the mystical strands and glue that tethered our minds to the universe. The spells she would need and use against Chandy were eked out of the nectar of knowledge, churned in the cauldron of universal truths from the ocean of world knowledge. Chackochan would stretch and frill the fabric of time. Learning became endless. Kusum was accomplishing years of learning every single light. Later, back in her room, she could compress a six-hour sleep cycle into an hour's snooze. Concoctions brewed by the Chathans made sleep superfluous to metabolic restoration.

Every morning, rested and restored she would be back at work. Kusum could sense the power growing with her. Soon Kusum could savor, grasp, and succor the glory of the universe. The last leg of the journey was the quest for self. Chackochan had first taught her to see within herself. The journey through her own self had taken her a fortnight to complete. She was initially embarrassed that everything in her life, including her relationship with Richard was an open book to her master. Once she knew herself, she learned to focus her powers. She could move objects with her mind, read others' thoughts, and influence their actions. The secret of great power is to keep one's power a secret. Chackochan had extolled. However, she had taken his permission to read Thomas' mind and see all the horrors he had been through. Cantering through his catastrophic memories he would benefit from the axonal reconnection and the emotional cleansing. His recovery was faster now. He could speak a few sentences soon. Kesavan was pleased at his master's recovery. Indeed, all their relatives attributed the recovery to Kesavan's loyal caregiving.

Meanwhile, the attacks and atrocities on various cities all over the globe continued unabated. There seemed to be a definite method in the madness. Ravaged by resource and revenue-sapping vengeful attacks and reprisals, one by one the economies of the Western powers crumbled. Futile strikes by powerful nations against perceived threats perversely made global tensions worse. After their night's visit, Chackochan had forbidden her from peeking into Chandy's vedic center. She was strong enough, but not strong enough to conceal her own strength. Chackochan and Kusum used the chathans for damage control. Some of the bombs placed by the terrorists in the densest population centers failed to explode. A school principal evacuated his five hundred wards to safety minutes before an explosion brought down the school building. Kusum's chathans were doing their bit. But as long as the masterminds remained free, attacks would continue.

<u>Fusion and Fission:</u>

Early in her training, Kusum had suggested that they get the security agencies involved.

Chackochan disagreed. Chandy was networked and had the backing of powerful people. Many powerful people who backed him did not realize the depth and spectrum of his operation. They labored under the delusion that Chandy was 'their man'. Chandy could read people's thoughts and scan their minds. He was constantly monitoring their attitudes. Long before any of them turned against him, he would know. It would be a simple matter to spirit away his close coterie to another place or even to decentralize the controls. The only way to restrain or stymie Chandy was from within his organization. Someone had to be smart enough to enter Chandy's circle of trust and immobilize it from within. Kusum soon realized that this was her job.

Chandy stopped coming to their church. He was busy and the church did not serve his purpose anymore. He still gave guest lectures at public conferences. Kusum decided to attend one of his talks at the Intercontinental Hotel in Kochi. She got herself invited through the management of one of the colleges she taught at. Kusum reached early. There was a reserved seat for her in the second row. She had not told Richard that she would be attending Chandy's talk. He would be unnecessarily worried. The hall was filling up quickly. She recognized many academics and thinkers. Chandy's philosophies were controversial. The concepts and conclusions he avowed were facile yet fascinating. Any talk by him evoked concern, consternation, and interest. You could accept or reject his tenets. You could not ignore him. His oratory and knowledge were exquisite.

There were many eminent professors in the audience. A few of them had come over to greet her. Kusum rarely attended public functions. People were pleasantly surprised at her presence. At seven PM, exactly on time, Chandy entered and walked straight to the podium. This was his style. He was intolerant of long introductions. His time was valuable. He stood straight and confident at the podium and started his discourse. There was a definite charisma about him. Kusum was impressed. She would need to remember Chackochan's warning. His insatiable appetite for surreal power was clad in the garb of academia and propped by a towering personality. Chandy was no cheap charlatan. His conviction in his own appeal and divinity was complete. He had been foiled twice in his bid to own and possess her. Kusum and the chathans she controlled were an obsession for Chandy. He would seek her vulnerability to possess and to demolish her will. Kusum steeled herself. To get his trust she had to hide her strength. Chandy should not realize how powerful she was.

Chandy was speaking about the unity of religions and of universal peace. The crowd cheered him as spoke of a new unified world order of synchronized convictions. The monster wants to take over the world, Kusum thought to herself. For almost an hour, Chandy held the audience spellbound. Then the lecture was over. His eyes scanned the crowd. His gaze was like a burning strong hand on her torso. His eyes seemed to gauge and gorge her modest defenses. There was an aura of victory and a hint of a smile at the corner of his mouth. The question-answer session was soon over. There was a small reception in his honor. As he was leaving, he stopped by Kusum's side. "I will drop you to your place," he said. "Her father-in-law is a very close friend of mine", he explained to his hosts. Kusum followed him to his car. He held the door open as Kusum got in. He closed the car door. Chandy then got into the driver's seat. He never used a chauffeur and preferred to drive himself.

Chandy negotiated the city traffic with characteristic elan. Soon they were outside town limits. He turned the car towards the high ranges. He had no intention of taking Kusum to her house. They were headed for his Vedic Center. They had not spoken a word in the car. Kusum could sense his animal magnetism. She sat firmly in her seat, her eyes on the road ahead. The car had tinted windows. They were shielded from the world's eye.

Chandy slowed down the car at the Vedic center's gates, punching in a security code on his car's keyboard. The gates swung open. She could see security guards on either side snap to attention as the car drove past them and into the woods. The road was narrow. There were no street lights. There was forest on both sides of the road. Chandy rolled down the windows to allow the sounds and smell of the forest in. An occasional deer peeked out as the car purred past. The road was isolated and there were no buildings by the way. The car slowed. Ahead of them was a cottage. Chandy stopped the car and held her door open as she got down. He held her arm as he opened the cottage door. The lighting inside was subdued. He pulled Kusum to him and kissed her on her mouth. She was powerless to resist his caresses. Her hands were round his neck and she clung to him as he undressed her. She locked her legs around his waist as he carried her up the stairs and to the bedroom. Her primeval moan shattered the still silence of the wood. Monkeys chattered in consternation and a flock of birds rose to the air from the tree near the bedroom window. Then there was silence except for their rasping breath. They slept a while, locked in a silent sweaty embrace. Kusum tried to keep her mind closed to what was happening. She had to win his confidence. His domination had to be complete and her surrender absolute. Chandy had folded her sari neatly on the dressing table. A long cool drink restored her. He was kissing her again.

The sun was shimmering in through the bedroom window blinds when Kusum woke up. Chandy had left for work. She was alone in the house. Donning a kaftan which had been laid out for her, she opened the windows wide. She could feel her body glow with sizzling energy. On the porch, there was a car and a chauffeur waiting for her. Kusum looked around. The room looked familiar. It had been designed for her tastes and her whims. There was a cupboard in the room. Inside she found clothes she could wear. Kusum had no idea, how he had managed to organize it, but the house seemed to have been tailored for her. She went down to the stacked kitchen and made herself breakfast. Later she went down to the car. The driver held the door open as she approached. The chauffeur had apparently been instructed to drive her around the premises before taking her to Chandy's office block.

The greenery was magnificent. They passed by the grounds she had seen with Chackochan. Kusum was grateful she was alone with the driver. If Chandy had been there, he may have sensed that she had seen this before. There were dozens of people in flowing white robs meditating in the shade under the trees. They were mostly foreigners, but a few Indians could be seen in the group. They passed the ground and drove through the forest path. There was a magnificent lake that seemed to stretch to the horizon. A waft of mist still lingered over the turquoise-blue water. At the far side of the lake was a rocky mountain face. The driver stopped the car. She walked over to the water's edge. She could hear a muffled roar in the distance. She squinted through the mist. In the distance, there was a waterfall cascading down the rock face of the mountain. A little distance away, there was a gap in the hills. A steady stream of mist was rising from the depths of the valley beyond. Kusum guessed that there was another waterfall in the valley.

It took them almost an hour to drive around the campus. Kusum guessed that there were some things Chandy had to clear up. Kusum was now driven down to the main office block. The office block was an impressive three-storied building. The architecture was unmistakably British. The high roofs and archways A polite attendant, dressed in pure white, escorted her to Chandy's office. When she entered, there were two people sitting with Chandy. One of them was dressed in the traditional robes of an Arab. The other was a burly white man, possibly a Russian, thought Kusum. They rose and excused themselves as she entered. Chandy rose, holding out his hand. Then, with his arm around her waist, he showed her around the area. The building was granite and red stone. The solid construction of British vintage. "This building was originally made for the English Viceroy", Chandy explained. We renovated it. Chandy guided her to a large hall. This was a library cum museum. Each wall of the hall seemed to be devoted to the history of a particular religion. There was a wall devoted to Hindu culture and Philosophy. A section was devoted to Buddhist studies. Christianity, Islam, and Judaism had their sections. The library was stacked. Most of the books seemed to be on history and philosophy. One whole cupboard was full of books written by Chandy.

On the first floor, they came across the conference hall, that Kusum recognized from her midnight visit. The great teak table with its heavy wooden chairs brought back memories of his visit with Chackochan. Kusum quickly blanked out her thoughts. The true Kusum would be kept hidden. She knew she would know when it was time to act.

Chandy had work in his office. Kusum retired to the library. She picked up a volume on the Crusades. She was reading history after a long time and to her present surprise, she was enjoying it. She was sitting, engrossed in her book when she felt a tap on her shoulder. She glanced at her watch. It was two in the afternoon. They went to their cottage for lunch. Chandy spends the afternoon with her. After tea, he left for the office again. There was a study in the cottage and to her surprise, she found it stacked with books on nuclear physics. Chandy had been very thoughtful.

Kusum had phoned Kesavan the previous night and lied to him that she was off to Bangalore for a talk. The telephone was working, but she was sure it was being monitored. There was an internet connection. Kusum telephoned Kesavan again. She would be away for a few days. She got out some books. She chalked out a timetable for herself. She sent a noncommittal mail to Richard. Chandy came back for dinner. After a while, he went back to the office. His capacity to work was stupendous and his work ethic was impeccable.

Kusum got back to work. The books were current and the internet connection was fast. She continued the paper she writing. She knew Chackochan would not contact her now. There could be nothing that would proffer Chandy even a whiff of suspicion. He must be conducting his nocturnal briefing, guessed Kusum. Kusum was awake when he got back home at three in the morning. He had glanced at all the papers and books strewn about the study and smiled.

In the morning, when she woke up, Chandy had left for work. Breakfast was on the table. There were sausages, some bread, and a boiled egg. Kusum liked continental breakfasts. She drank her coffee and changed into a sporty attire from her well-stocked cupboard. On the porch, the car was waiting. Today she would do an hour of boating before going to the library. A small sailboat had been kept ready for her. The attendant at the club gave her tips on rigging the boat and a few initial lessons in sailing. Later she went to the library till lunchtime. The days went by. She had learned to take out a sailboat and had undergone yoga lessons. The review article on Bosons, which she planned to submit for publication was almost complete.

Chandy had not taken her along for any of his evening meets. Then one evening, as he was leaving, he asked her. "Would you like to come along with me". Silently she changed and got ready. The car was waiting downstairs with its engine running. In front of the main building, there were a dozen large cars parked. There was something major in the offing. "In the next two weeks, the world as you know it will change completely", he told Kusum.

The gathering got to its feet as they entered. Chandy sat at the head of the conference table. Kusum sat on a smaller chair, a few paces behind. The men in the room represented diverse cultures. There were hardened and seasoned veterans of myriad mercenary outfits. There were pressmen who looked vaguely familiar. On giant screens adorning the walls were recognizable international participants. A video conference was in the offing. Kusum looked around at the TV screens. She realized she would have seen their faces in the newspapers. She recognized the proprietor of an international news network. There was a technology baron whose interest and acquisitions in generative AI and robotics had caused consternation in world military circles. The deliberations started. Kusum was getting bits and pieces of information. The jigsaw puzzle was slowly filling up. There was a major operation in the offing. Chandy was reassuring one of the worried-looking Arab delegates. "The plutonium is safe, on an island, a hundred miles from the nearest shore. The gifts have already been wrapped". On the screen, he flashed a slide. There was a ball, the size of an apple concealed within a toy dog, gift-wrapped in a box. "The gifts will be delivered three days from now".

Someone else had asked a question and Chandy was elaborating. "The island is manned by the fiercest guardians, you have ever seen", he said. Only I and she have any control over them. The others looked at Kusum. They all seemed to know about her. "So this was where the Chathans in Chandy's control were". With their magical powers, they could certainly slip past any check post. She tried to imagine how much destruction these balls of plutonium could unleash. There would be Mayhem. Millions would die. There would be inevitable retaliatory attacks as nations struck out in anguish. Retaliatory attacks against imagined and unknown enemies would embroil civilization in death throes, thought Kusum. The masterminds in the Vedic Center would wait till the dust settled. She was looking more closely at the men around the table. They were all world figures. Factional leaders, tyrannical politicians a few bearded guerillas. They were soon discussing their plans for a new order. With so much destruction, there would be a great vacuum and these men had in place the philosophy, the men, and the machinery, fine-tuned in detail, to fill it.

At around three in the morning, Chandy halted the deliberations. There would be sub-committees to fine-tune details. It was best to give people only relevant information and necessary orders. The meeting ended. Chandy was a visionary, charismatic, and effective leader. The tragedy was that his vision and mission were warped. He never micromanaged. It was not worthwhile discussing trivial details. Kusum and Chandy returned to the cottage. The lights were dimmed and the water in the bath was warm. Chandy was very intense. Kusum reciprocated. She seized the initiative and savored the sensations. She knew this would be her last night with Chandy.

The next morning, by the time Kusum got up, Chandy had already left. She got ready early. There was a plan evolving in her mind. Kusum sat and meditated for an hour. He garnered her mental strings. Soon she was the old Kusum again. She was pleasantly surprised that her mental powers had not been dented with the time she had spent with Chandy. It had been necessary. In the car, she told the driver to take her to the lake. She would go sailing today.

At the sailing club, the attendant rigged up the boat for her. It was a pleasant day. She could take the boat out on her own. The lake water was placid and cool. A light wind puffed the sails as she sailed towards the waterfalls. The attendant would be watching her through his binoculars. If she got into any trouble, he would reach her with his speed boat in a few minutes.

In half an hour she was closer to the waterfall. Here the lake was at its deepest. The spray from the waterfall hovered like a fine mist over the blue water. The boat station attendant would be worried now. If she sailed any closer to the waterfall he would start his motorboat and zoom over. It was time to act. Kusum closed her eyes and meditated.

Huge black clouds seemed to appear out of nowhere. The wind picked up. The placid surface of the lake had suddenly turned choppy. In her mind's eye, she watched as the attendant ran towards the rescue boat. A large wave picked up the boat and dashed it against the pier. There was a hole in its hull and water was gushing in The frantic attendant was rushing back to the boat pool to get another boat. He was shouting into his radio. Hail and rain made the visibility dismal. She could barely see her hand in front of her face. Quickly she stripped off her outer clothes. A swirl of wind lifted her from the boat, cradling her in its cold arms. Her boat had disappeared beneath the waterfall. There was a crash as the mast came down.

Kesavan heard sounds of someone moving about in Kusum's room. He went to the door. It was latched from the inside. "Who is it?" he asked, suddenly frightened. "It is me", it was Kusum's voice. "When did you come, I did not see you". "I got wet, you were too busy watching the rain," said Kusum smiling to herself. She had changed into a dry set of clothes and opened the door. She sat and talked to Thomas for a while, as Kesavan got some tea and biscuits ready. Outside, the fierce storm was settling down. Some trees had been uprooted by the hurricane. Fortunately, the house had not been damaged. It was almost time for lunch. Kusum smiled as she reminisced. There would be a massive search operation going on in the Vedic center. It would take them days to fish out the ruins of her sailboat from under the waterfall. She knew that Chandy would go ahead with his plans. There was not much time. Thomas retired to his room after lunch. Kesavan too would rest for a while. Kusum walked to her study and latched it from inside. She climbed the stairs to the loft.

To her surprise Chackochan was already there, and so were some of the others she had met before. If they were meeting so early in the day, it meant that time was crucial. They all rose from their chairs as Kusum entered. Chackochan put an arm around her. You are a good student, he said. You exceed your master in your powers. We are proud of you. The Chathans got them tea and snacks. The meeting was on.

On Chackochan's instruction, a screen was rigged up by Tinku. A projector had been installed in the loft which had transformed into a conference hall. There was a map of the earth with the cities, where terrorist strikes had occurred flagged in red. The next slide showed a group of islands off the coast of Africa. The slide zoomed down on one of the islands. This, said Chackochan is where the plutonium stolen from various reactors all over the world is kept. It is more than a hundred miles from the mainland. He pointed to the map of the African continent. We all know that a military base has been set up on the coastline by an emergent African nation with democratic pretensions, oil reserves, and territorial aspirations. He now pointed to the island beyond. A naval base has been set up here by a superpower. In between these two bases, the island is invincible by conventional methods. The island itself is guarded by a small contingent of troops with radiation protection suits. The actual handling of the Plutonium however is by the Chathans in Chandy's control. The plutonium has been packaged and is ready for distribution. Kusum nodded. She had seen the photographs during Chandy's briefing.

Kusum turned to Tinku. Can you get to the island and destroy those gifts? Tinku looked down. Chandy had cast a powerful spell around the island. No chathan would get on or off except the five in his control. Chackochan flashed another slide. There was a map of the world again. There were stars over five major cities in the world. These were the targets for the plutonium bombs.

"When is the plutonium going to be moved from the island", Kusum asked Chackochan. "Possibly early tomorrow morning", was the answer. Chackochan looked at Kusum. She rose. The time for deliberation was over. Now it was time to act. Kusum went down from the loft. She went to her room and changed into jeans and a dark pullover. Thomas was getting up. "I have to go to Bangalore again, urgently", she told him. Thomas nodded. Kusum wondered as to how much he knew. She had a feeling that Thomas knew more than he made out. He was of Chackochan's 'Blood Line' and had inherited his genome. Thomas put his hand on Kusum's head and closed his eyes in silent prayer. She hugged him and left. A car was drawn up for her outside. Tossing in an overnight bag she hopped in. The driver appeared unfamiliar. He turned around and winked at her. Kusum smiled. It was Chackochan. He knew what had to be done.

They drove straight to the harbor. A yacht was waiting for her, its engines revved. Up the gangway, she went. A young captain received her at the top. The yacht cast off. A smiling sailor escorted her to the owner's cabin by the flight deck. Another carried her bag. She opened the door and gasped in surprise.

Seated in the cabin, facing her, was Richard. The sailors left. Richard embraced her. My grandfather kept me abreast of all that was going on, he said. There was a map in the cabin. A green dot on the map showed them, where they were. A miniature, solar-powered, Beetle-shaped drone, on loan from DARPA had been deployed to decipher and track Chandy's moves. On their map, a red flag would tag the movements of Chandy and his troops.

The boat was soon in the open sea and heading straight for the islands. There was a slight snap as the boat skimmed up on its silvery foils. The ship's captain made some rough calculations. The islands would be visible early next morning. Richard updated her on what was going on. Chandy had left the Vedic center earlier than scheduled. The search for Kusum's body was still on with submersibles and scuba divers. They had found the wrecked boat under the waterfall.

Chandy and the other operation leaders were now in an aircraft heading for Africa. They flew in a corporate executive jet loaned from a billionaire businessman. The airplane would land at Mombasa. A military aircraft would then transport them to the naval base. They would control operations from there. With Chandy moving early, he would be upon the islands hours before Kusum and Richard. Every second was crucial. It was probable that he would activate his plans at the earliest. It would be touch and go. Richard had no idea, as to how Kusum intended to wreck Chandy's plan. Even Chackochan and his grandfather were clueless about her plans. Kusum seemed to have synched with the essence of earth. She was in concord with the forces of nature and her strategy would evolve with ebb and flow of the pulse of the earth. Robert did not disturb her with prattle. He was just an instrument, a charioteer, a krishna to Kusum's Arjun. The elders had just instructed him to get her close to the island. She would think up something. The timing was crucial. With Chandy in position at the Naval base, the operation would start. Once the plutonium left the island, it would be difficult to stop their delivery.

Kusum walked up the sundeck. The boat had its hydrofoils down and was skimming across the water at high speed. Kusum picked up a chair and sat at the center of the deck. Richard saw that she was meditating. Unobtrusively he picked up a deck chair and sat a distance away, watching her. He could sense her powerful synchronized synergy with the sea and the waves. Far away, he could see a pillar of rain. As he watched in awed amazement, the storm seemed to be heading in the same direction as the boat. The tempest was soon moving much faster and was strumming with a subdued roar as it raced to the faraway shore. A throbbing tower of water sucked up from the seas, spewed sizzling water and shoals of fish like a giant festive fountain. He realized that Kusum had raised the cyclone. He realized what she was doing. Chandy's aircraft would not be able to land in time. She had bought them a few crucial hours.

Kusum turned around. She was smiling. She is comfortable with her great power now and senses that Richard knows it. Their boat surged forward riding the storm's symphonic surf. They rang for the steward and had a light dinner on deck. The storm subsided as abruptly as it had started. It was a moonless night, there were dark clouds all over. A few stars peeked out in curious consternation to wink and to dim and deceive before being shielded and shrouded by the fury of darkness again. After dinner, they retired to the cabin. They would sleep till morning. The next day would be eventful.

Chandy felt discombobulated. An unexpected storm had shut down the airport where their private jetliner was to land. Chandy was furious. Too many unexpected events had occurred for comfort. Kusum's boat accident, due to the sudden storm which came from nowhere had jolted him. The plutonium bombs were to be distributed after he and his men had taken position in the military base. Now, with the weather playing up again, the whole program would be delayed. The men with him were veterans. They had all risen through the ranks of turmoil and terror. They were used to the unexpected. Yet Chandy had a growing sense of unease. There were some powerful forces in action he could not pinpoint. With Kusum under his control, he had the feeling that he was unstoppable. It was only a matter of time before he controlled all the Chathans. He would need them to enforce a new world order after the dust settled from tomorrow's operations. Now Kusum was gone. They were in radio communication with the military base. The program would kick off after he reached the control center. His Chathans were unstoppable delivery boys. But he would control them personally.

The geographic and strategic location of the islands was unique and indomitable. On the mainland was a military dictatorship loyal to Chandy. Across the island was another group of islands where a sympathetic superpower had created a naval base. Chandy had been facilitative and instrumental in their choice of location for a base. With this kind of protection, not even a dolphin could reach his island without Chandy's permission. Getting the plutonium had taken time. The Chathans had to get the material from various reactors without exciting suspicion. But now it was all ready. In the next 48 hours, a fair share of the population of five major metros would be annihilated. In the retributions and counter-retributions to follow, many more countries and cities would be razed to the ground. Chandy's men had networked into the fourth estate. Through an AI-powered misinformation campaign, they would tailor and chaperone the chaos in concord with the strategy. Chandy pondered over the extreme weather vicissitudes they encountered. The sudden storms were inexplicable. Were they part of some global change? He wondered if the nuclear explosions he planned would make the weather even more unpredictable. There have been more earthquakes and volcanic eruptions in the past decade than ever before in history. Chandy's islands were part of a submerged volcanic chain. Fortunately, these volcanoes had been dormant for centuries. Their pilot had taken a detour. Their airplane landed in a military airstrip a thousand kilometers away. Logistic support from the military organization was impeccable. A fleet of limousines with a military escort was waiting for them. They would drive cross country to the base and then proceed by boat to their control center.

Kusum and Richard had breakfast in the Cabin. They would be in the vicinity of the island group before midday. At around eleven 'o'clock the captain called them to his control deck. The naval base was around two hundred nautical miles away. A reconnaissance aircraft had already flown over them a couple of times. On the radar, they could see a group of dots heading toward the base. "Yachts and small offshore patrol boats, judging from their size and speed". said the captain. The Island was receiving visitors. Kusum guessed that Chandy and his group would be in one of the boats. A boat had broken ranks from the group and was heading towards their yacht. Soon the patrol boat could be seen at the horizon.

It was a fast offshore patrol vessel, bristling with guns. It drew alongside. A search party came on board. They searched the yacht. No one in the search party paid attention to Kusum or Richard. They were looking for arms or a concealed commando group. The yacht was clean. It seemed to be a rich playboy taking his girl out for a romantic cruise. "This is a military exercise area", the young officer warned. Turn around and stay away from here. The patrol boat left.

Their captain was looking to them for instructions. If they detoured the islands, further north was a civilian harbor. They studied the map. Kusum pointed toward a cove there. Take us here, she told the captain. Their vessel altered course. They reached the natural port in a couple of hours. Kusum and Richard took a boat to the beach which seemed uninhabited. On their instructions, the Captain turned the yacht around and headed away. He should put as much distance between himself and the naval base as possible, Kusum had exhorted. The captain understood. All hell was going to burst loose.

Chandy and the other leaders reached the control center. It was quite late in the day. They held a council of war. Chandy was of the opinion that they should deploy the bombs straightaway. But the others urged restraint. Even if they deployed the gifts immediately, it would be midnight in at least two of the cities when the explosion took place. Most people would be indoors and the city centers would not be brimming with crowds. Besides, it would take a few hours of fine-tuning for operational synchrony to be complete. Reluctantly Chandy had agreed. They spent the rest of the day briefing their teams. The Chathans would leave the island with their radioactive loads by six in the morning. In six hours, they would be in position. There would be a conventional diversionary attack by a group of suicide bombers at this time. Press reporters would be zooming in on this event when the serial nuclear explosions started. The attack and the nuclear explosions would be linked by the press to provide a pattern. A pattern that would provoke a nuclear retaliation by the West.

Chandy remained at his control console, listening in and symphonizing the fine detail. The operation was now ready for execution. Every detail had been meticulously analyzed. Chandy rang up his aides at the Vedic Center. Kusum's body had not been found, but the jacket she had worn and tattered shards of the boat's sail had been retrieved from beneath the waterfall. There was another disturbing report. One of the Chandy's men had seen a lady in a dark pullover, dark glasses, and a cap, who looked like Kusum embark a private yacht. Chandy asked for the yacht's identification. There had been a similar yacht that had been turned away from the area by a patrol boat. Chandy's antennae were humming in distress. He summoned the Captain of the vessel which intercepted and searched the yacht. The yacht was clean, there were no guns or bombs, but yes, there were a couple on board. Chandy retrieved photos of Richard and Kusum from his archives. The Captain identified them. It was Richard and Kusum. Chandy realized that all his plans were under threat. He barked an order to his attaché.

In a trice, he was in the control room. The other leaders had been summoned urgently, some of them yanked out of bed. Chandy had decided to deploy immediately. He had underestimated Kusum. Her physical subjugation to him had been a ploy to lull him into a false sense of security. Kusum was alive. She had powers that surpassed his. If he did not act now, she would subvert the whole operation, thought Chandy. The military base had crackled to life. His Chathans were lined up in front of him getting their final orders. He had driven an additional nail into each of their heads. They were now like programmed bombs. No one, not even Kusum or other Chathans could deter them from their tasks. They were unstoppable. The parcels were ready and the Chathans were ready to move. Chandy felt a great relief. His plan would work. Kusum would be too late to prevent the carnage. His finger hovered over a control button that would ignite the operations. The table and control panel seemed to dance away from his finger. He grabbed Mike and flicked on the emergency switch.

Then he felt it. The earth seemed to be trembling. For a moment he thought he was unwell. Objects were crashing to the ground all around him. It was an earthquake. Through the window, he looked towards his islands. A plume of smoke had erupted towards the sky. A cloud of molten lava had spread like a purple mushroom cloud propped up by a dozen pillars of flames from the hills. The sky was blotted out and the spreading cloud was glimmering with a light and life of its own. He watched in fascination. The volcano on his island had erupted. All around him, men were running for cover as huge molten boulders crashed down around them. Chandy rushed towards the airstrip. There was a helicopter standing, still undamaged. He got in and started the rotors. The helicopter rose slowly through the cloud of dust. He headed towards his island. He was desperate. He would deliver the plutonium himself. He stared in disbelief as he lowered the helicopter below the veil of dust. His island had disappeared. The volcano had exploded and the island with its precious load of plutonium had disappeared beneath the sea bed.

Chandy knew that Kusum had somehow engineered this. His life's work lay in ruins. He had been bested by a girl who had gotten through his impenetrable fortress of fortitude with visage of vulnerability. Chandy's only thought was of revenge. Kusum was somewhere close by. He sensed her presence on the coast further north. He pointed his aircraft to where he sensed she would be. His helicopter seemed magically immune to the debris and lava, flying all about him. He was a man with a purpose, protected by the forces of evil.

After the yacht sped off, Kusum settled down on the beach and meditated. Richard stood guard. The beach was deserted, but the area around was a thick tropical forest. He was unarmed. He fashioned himself a spear with his penknife and walked up and down the beach at the edge of the jungle. It had grown dark, but the moon provided a semblance of light. In a while, the moon would set and darkness would be complete. He could feel the tremors as the earth shook beneath his feet. At the horizon, in the direction of Chandy's island, he could see a plume of smoke extending to the skies. His first concern was that the nuclear weapons had exploded. He could feel the splashes and thuds as molten boulders landed and sizzled the sea. This was not a nuclear holocaust. He realized that it was a volcanic explosion. Fortunately, a strong wind was blowing the rocks and debris away from them. Kusum was seated in a rock still engrossed in her powerful spell. Suddenly Richard noticed something amiss.

The sea was receding. The waters were being drawn back, baring the corralled nakedness of the ocean floor. He watched fascinated as flashes of incendiary orange painted lurid writhing throes on the sea bed. Abruptly he snapped out of his reverie. Far away he could hear a noise. It sounded like a speeding express train whooshing through a tunnel. On the horizon, he saw the wave. At first sight, it did not seem ominous. The wave was growing. As it neared the shallow seas it would grow. Richard realized that he was seeing a Tsunami in rapid evolution. As the wave neared the shore it would take the full proportions of a tidal wave. This was a tidal wave triggered by the underwater seismic activity. Shouting, he ran towards Kusum. She was unconscious. The powerful magic had drained her completely. Picking up her limp body in his arms he ran into the forest. He could see deer and elephants running away from the water's edge. All the animals were trying to reach the safety of the hills behind.

He was racing up the hill when he heard a sickening crash as a thundering mountain of water descended upon the shoreline. He could hear the creaks and crashes as trees in the forest snapped like matchsticks. The wave had caught up with him now, but he kept moving uphill. There was a crest ahead. He hoisted Kusum over and heaved himself up. He kept moving uphill. Kusum was cradled in his arms. He was halfway up the hill. The waters had caught up and soon were swirling around his chest. He was sure that they were going to drown. There was a pause in the torrent as Mother Nature patted the angry wave down. An eerie silence signaled that the wave had stopped. A new sound started. It was as though a giant flush had been pulled by an irate, unknown giant. The water was receding again. The sea was sucked back into its vortex the debris and detritus along its path of destruction in an eerie attempt to conceal the consequences of its tempestuous temper tantrum. Richard was being swept off his feet and he and Kusum weres being sucked back into the sea. There was a tree nearby and he held on to it with one hand, the other holding Kusum tightly as the waters growled and gushed back. It was all over in a few minutes. Richard looked back with disbelief. The forest below had been flattened as if by a giant lawn mower. The tree he had held on to was one of the few still standing. Behind him, further up the hill the forest bridled with anguish. The sea, ignited by a flood of molten lava, was boiling as it swirled like a simmering soup in a giant brimming earthen bowl. Branches littered the ocean surface for as far as he could see.

Richard gently laid Kusum down on the grass. She was still deeply unconscious. There was a trickle of blood and froth coming out of her nose and mouth. She lay immobile. Richard felt her pulse. It was racing a rapid gallop with occasional pauses and resets. He checked her eyes. Both her pupils were dilated but her eyes moved rhythmically. It was almost as though she were recovering from an epileptic attack. There was a rustle in the forest behind. Richard heard a roar. He turned around and his blood froze. There was a pride of lions there, licking each other dry. For the moment, they seemed preoccupied. But would they turn on the two helpless humans? Richard heard a hum in the distance. He looked up at the sky and saw a helicopter. Taking off his shirt, he waved it frantically. The pilot seemed to see them. He seemed to alter course towards them. The copter landed about 10 yards away from them. Richard got up thankfully, his face beaming in relief. Kusum was still unconscious. Lifting her in his arms, he walked crouched down towards the helicopter. It was dark now, the moon had disappeared beneath the horizon. The door of the helicopter swung open and a man emerged. He held a pistol in his hands.

Even in the dark, Richard could make out that it was Chandy. Numbed, Richard sat down as Chandy strolled over and kicked him on the jaw. Then, aiming his gun at Richards's leg, he fired. Richard felt a shooting pain as the bullet seared through his calf, glancing off the bone. "That is to make sure you don't run away till I finish with her", said Chandy. He caught hold of Kusum's hair and dragged her towards the bush. Richard tried to move, but his leg was ablaze with a thousand arrows of pain. He saw Chandy take a hunting knife and rip through Kusum's pullover. Suddenly there was a roar. There was a scream of fright from Chandy as the lion pounced on him, knocking him to the ground. Another lion caught his leg and dragged him to the bushes. Kusum had woken up with pain as Chandy dragged her by the hair through the clearing. She felt a trickle of blood down her chest as he sliced her blouse open with his hunting knife. Then the lions attacked. She lay there limp as they tore into Chandy in the bushes a few feet away. They dragged him further away into the undergrowth.

She was sure they would come back for her, but they did not. She could hear Richard moaning in the distance. She crept towards him. He had lost a lot of blood and was almost delirious with shock. Whipping off her tattered pullover she tied it tightly around his leg to staunch the bleeding. Richard opened his eyes. She kissed him on his forehead transferring and imparting some of her vital energy. Then slowly, she helped him pull himself into the helicopter. Kusum propped him up on the co-pilot's seat. Richard was a qualified helicopter pilot. Kusum was confident she could fly the plane if he would help her. Richard smiled. Kusum's strength had returned. She would get them back to civilization. Kusum was mustering his strength to help her. At his orders, she flicked the power on. They started the helicopter's rotors. It was still dark. Over the horizon, gleams of orange sunlight heralded the onset of a new dawn. The helicopter rose through plumes of smoke-tinged sunbeams. "Keep following the coastline", Richard instructed her. On his radio, he called for the captain of their yacht. To their left, volcanic ash was settling down on the sea surface coloring it a brilliant orange. An occasional gush of steam still shot up from the depths of the ocean.

They studied the sea below in the flickering beams of a new dawn. The volcanic eruption was by and large contained. Chandy's island had been swallowed and buried under tons of molten rock. Kusum was getting the feel of flying. Having Richard by her side gave her confidence. They pointed the helicopter south tethering their course to the thin line of pulsing froth where waves licked an abraded beach. The sun was now rising up in the morning sky. Kusum gave a shout of relief. Ahead, in the water, a few hundred meters from the shore, they saw their yacht. Richard took over the controls as they settled the helicopter down on the sandy beach.

The yacht's boat was already in the water, heading for them. On board the yacht, Kusum examined Richard's leg. The bullet had not fractured the tibia, but the fibula was broken. Fortunately, the arterial pulses in the foot were good. Movements of the ankle and toe seemed to be normal. Richard could sense her touch his foot. She was sure the leg would heal. The yacht had a well-equipped first aid kit. She washed out his wound well with a disinfectant and applied a sterile dressing. They gave him an injectable antibiotic and a painkiller. On Richard's request, they carried him up to the sundeck and let him lie there. Kusum sat by his side, holding his hand. A flurry of flying fish raced their boat as they cruised towards south India.

<u>Epilogue</u>

Kusum finished dinner with Thomas and Kesavan. On the TV screen in front of them, images of the volcanic eruption in the Arabian Sea were flashing. A naval base had been destroyed, but there were no civilian casualties.

They had admitted Richard to the Kochi hospital. The orthopedic team had echoed Kusum's evaluation. The flesh wound caused by the bullet would heal without problems. He would be out, hobbling on crutches in a week's time. Richard will be moving to Kerala soon. The International Institute of Technological Studies was establishing an Asian center in Kerala. They had purchased the premises of the Center for Vedic Studies. Richard would be the director, Kusum had been offered the post of Dean. She decided to accept the offer.

Thomas and Kesavan had retired for the night. Kusum played with the dogs for a while and then went to her study. She had to plan the course syllabi and appoint faculty for the center. The clock was chiming midnight when she looked up from her work. The study door had wafted open. She followed Chackochan up the stairs to the loft. The conference hall had appeared again, one last time. Richard's grandfather and the others were there. They raised a toast to her. The fruit wine was delicious. The Chathan's had dressed up in all their finery to serve for this banquet. The war had been won. Good has triumphed over evil again. There would be peace and prosperity now for a few hundred years more.

One by one. the old men came and embraced her before leaving. Chackochan was the last to leave. The Chathans would be around in the loft whenever she needed them. The hall disappeared. The loft was, as she remembered it from earlier. They shifted the box back into the corner. Tinku handed her the boxes key again. Outside, a few birds chirped. Kusum retired to bed. She would wake up to a new life, a new dawn. Tinku and the Chathans tucked her in. They could rest now, counting waves, chasing flying fish, and blowing occasional storms out.

Contents